Also by Nancy Frederick

Touring the Afterlife
A Change of Heart
Starstruck
The Sportin' Life

The Astro Tutor
Love and Sex Under the Stars
The Lover's Dream
Love Games: Psychic Paths to Love
Palmistry: All Lines Lead to Love
Tarot: Love is in the Cards

ACKNOWLEDGMENTS

Thanks so much to my editorial black belt friends Jack Pettey and Steven Darancette for offering suggestions, corrections, and advice about this manuscript. I appreciate all your Ninja stealth in ridding me of my lamebrain mistakes.

Hungry for Love

Nancy Frederick

The kids were fighting as they did every morning at the car. There were screams about who was to ride up front, words like shotgun, insults like poptart. Candy, who was only eight, was screaming, "When is it my turn to be older? I want it to be my turn."

Normally by now Dr. Bill Masters would have focused on the fracas and broken it up but he didn't even hear his son Will chortle and cruelly say, "Never. Exactly never is when you'll be older. Not even when we're both dead." Normally Bill would have stepped between his warring children and made a joke to set their minds at ease. By now he would have hugged Candy, who was weeping, and he would have set a stern but kind hand on his son's shoulder. But he was distracted. There was a woman coming out of his house in running clothes and she carried two brown lunch bags. That wasn't JoEllen. It looked like her though.

Bill shook his head like a dog tossing off some water. It didn't work. He still felt damp and fuzzy. The woman locked the door — she had a key — and walked over to him. Suddenly his brain snapped awake. This was Chrissy and she was his live in girlfriend. For a year. What was wrong with him today?

"Forget your lunches, kids?" Chrissy smiled and tossed the lunches in the front seat, kissed Bill casually, and ran down the street, her voice floating back like music over a fence, "Have a slender day!"

"What?" said Bill. He turned to watch Chrissy run off and saw his dumpling of an old lady neighbor waving at him. Bill walked toward Sophie Gold as the kids continued to struggle over who would get to sit up front.

"Check me out, Dr. M." said Sophie, striking a pose in her velour sweat suit. "I'm back down to fighting weight, thanks to you. Made it all the way around the block today."

"Great work, Mrs. G. Where's Mr. G? Why isn't he walking with you?"

"If Bert were here how could I flirt with you?" she laughed. "I'm planning to bring you some of my strudel later today. Gotta sneak it in when that one isn't looking." She gestured toward where Chrissy was disappearing into the distance. She patted Bill's cheek and sighed, "Oh so cute. If only I were a week or two younger."

Bill laughed. "You'd be too much woman for me, Mrs. G, we both know that."

She nodded in agreement. "I'd take it easy on you, but only at first."

"Oh you're just shameful. And what would Mr. G say? He's not a gun collector is he?"

"He'd say go on, take my wife. But leave the strudel."

Bill laughed only for a second until Mrs. G pointed toward the kids, who were involved in an athletic shoving match, which of course Will was winning. "Get Mr. G in on the exercise," Bill said, waving as he walked back to the car.

"He has a good heart and a bad ticker," Sophie sighed, turning to return to her front door.

"Kids!" said Bill, "C'mon already. Every single day. Candy, you know you sit in the back. Kids your age have to sit in the back. It's safer. So that's the rule. When you're ten, you'll take turns, okay?"

"Not okay." Candy scowled and scrambled into the front seat anyway, snatching the brown bags and dumping out the contents. Will was about to grab her by the waist and pull her back out but Bill held up a hand to stop him.

"Dadeeeee," Candy whined, "Look at this." She held up two cans of Slimfast, pulled from the brown bags.

"Not again!" said Will.

Bill shook his head and settled the kids into the car. "We'll stop for something."

"She seemed so normal when we first started dating her," asserted Candy.

"I miss those days," said Will, sighing like an old man longing for the distant past.

Bill drove down his beautiful street, observing lush flowers on every lawn and noting that he should do some work in his own yard, neglected now for a couple of years. He pulled into a McDonald's and parked the car.

"Wow," said Candy, "McDonald's for breakfast again. My stomach is glowing with joy."

"Your mother would kill me," said Bill. "We'd better hurry though."

As they sat eating, Bill observed Candy squirming in her seat and looking at him as though something very weighty plagued her. She opened her mouth once or twice then shut it again. Finally he said, "Something on your mind, Toots?"

Candy gulped. She mumbled. She took a big swig of her milk. She opened her mouth. She took another gulp. Then she said, "Now Daddy I don't want you to hate me or anything."

"What," said Bill, astonished. "Hate you? My best sweetheart? You know better." He put his arm around her and squeezed her shoulders tightly, his dark eyes smiling.

"I've been thinking about this for a while, Daddy, and I really think we have to break up with Chrissy."

Will opened his eyes widely, glanced up to the ceiling, grimaced, then began eating with a feigned level of deep concentration.

"You do?" asked Bill. "Why's that?"

"It's the man pause," said Candy.

"Man pause?" asked Bill, smiling.

"Yes, Jessica's mom said girls have to get married young because soon enough the man pause comes and then you know what happens."

"What happens?" asked Will. This was a new subject to him.

"Well," said Candy seriously, "Just like it sounds. The men pause and don't ask the girl out any more. Chrissy has been acting crazy lately cause she's afraid of the man pause. Cause Daddy would never marry her. Then she'll have man pause and no husband."

"Why do you think I would never marry her?" asked Bill.

"Footwear," said Candy with conviction. "Jessica explained it to me."

"What?" asked Bill.

"Your soles have to be a mate. She's always in sneakers working out and your shoes are black."

"Yeah well Jessica is right for once. No way Chrissy is Dad's soulmate," said Will.

Bill looked at his children silently and thought for a while. "Maybe Chrissy is a little stressed about getting older. It's her birthday in a few weeks, but she's only thirty-four—nowhere near man pause." He laughed. "Maybe we could all be a little more understanding, show her we care. Why don't we try that."

Candy looked worried. "Okay Daddy I can try that but I don't see how that fixes the shoe problem."

"Maybe not," said Bill. "C'mon, let's get you to school."

After giving the kids money for lunches and dropping them off at their exclusive school, Bill knew he should head into the office. Patients would be waiting. But he did first what he often chose to do instead, stop off to see JoEllen. He knew it made no sense to be visiting her grave daily. She'd been gone nearly three years. He was with someone new. He was allowed to be happy again. Every single day he reminded himself of that—he was allowed to be happy again.

He stood there silently, yet another bouquet of roses in his hands. Had he bought JoEllen more roses when she was alive and the love of his life or now, since she was stony, silent, and completely unreachable? He didn't know.

Softly he said, "How am I supposed to live in the moment, when I never expected to live without you? That's what I want to know. But will you answer me?

Nope. Never. And you used to be such a chatterbox. You hated that didn't you. You said don't call me that, call me loquacious, it sounds smarter."

Bill stood there for a while, just trying to feel JoEllen around him, but all he could feel was the memories. He sighed deeply and under his breath he said, "I feel like a guy who was at the best party ever, then for no good reason his gal ditches him way too early and he's stuck trying to make do with all the other guests. I just wish you'd come to your senses and come back. But no, Jesus you're not."

Already at the Beverly Hills Wellness and Weight Loss Center, Bill's partner, Dr. Kevin Flicker, was in his office but not at his desk. Patients sat outside, either impatient to be congratulated on the week's current slimmer status or morose about the lack of same. Soon enough they would be weighed in and sent on their way, hopefully to return a little lighter the following week. Kevin and Bill had a good practice, mostly consisting of die hard dieters but also the occasional patient who wasn't fat and had the flu.

Inside Flicker's office there were stacks of unopened medical journals piled in a corner. An impressive mahogany desk was centered in the room and on it sat a collection of the desk toys Kevin favored. There was a nice tufted leather couch, so standard medical office that it was almost a cliché, and it would have been perfectly suitable for Kevin's current activity, except because his partner lacked the good grace to knock before entering his office, Kevin had become furtive, which actually added to the cheap thrills.

At the back of the office was a small closet, with a fairly solid wood door, a door which now shimmied rhythmically with a thud-thud-thud sound that was the backdrop for the muffled moans coming from behind it. Moan-thud-shimmy was the cadence. Slowly the sounds began to subside and the door opened. Nurse Caryn exited first, jiggling her breasts back into her bra and zipping up her uniform top. Kevin followed her, zipping up his fly with a flourish that was comical in its grandeur.

As Caryn turned to exit the office, Kevin reached out and pulled her toward him for a kiss. Then they both giggled. Life was good in Beverly Hills.

Not far from the Beverly Hills Wellness and Weight Loss Center, Kevin Flicker's most devoted—and determined—patient, a formerly fat, very fat, moderately fat, and now barely fat girl of twenty-six named Angie sat in a hairdresser's chair having microscopic slivers snipped off the ends of her lush and tastefully streaked hair. Next to her was Ben, her oldest friend, squeamishly squirming as though he were about to have a vasectomy rather than a dye job. What was being done to him didn't match his image at all. He'd worn cords almost since birth, even in the summer, and his thick glasses gave him a sort of New York intellectual look which in Beverly Hills made him resemble an actor in costume for a role.

Peering up hopefully, like a death row inmate waiting for that governor's reprieve, Ben mumbled, "This is a bad idea. Maybe we should stop." Looking more complacent than aghast, the hairdresser stepped back from Ben's chair and raised her arms in a gesture usually reserved for one of those contestants on a timed cooking competition, until Angie signaled to her to resume working. Ben's hair was enrobed in tin foil, and dye was painted on as he watched in the mirror with a grim look that suggested his next stop would be at an appliance store that sold beard and head trimmers that could cue ball him back into acceptability.

"Nobody will trust a shrink with streaky hair," he said solemnly.

"You see all your clients on the Internet or the phone, so why not. For all they know you wear a bozo wig and consult them naked."

Ben gasped, then returned his worried glance to the mirror. Haltingly he said, "And you don't think I'm gonna look silly?"

Angie smiled at him in the same way adults do when placating a difficult child. "No silly, I think you're gonna look hot and studly."

Ben perked up instantly then braved the subject he really wanted to discuss, "I feel like I should make you stop seeing him."

"Ahh Ben," sighed Angie, sweetly reaching out and squeezing his hand, "You're such a good pal, but I'll be just fine, so don't worry about me, okay?"

"But how can you just ignore your history? If you don't remember, I'm right here to remind you. Do you really want another incendiary incident, more embarrassment? C'mon. Remember Chef Raul? Remember...."

Angie's mind was lost then, floating back in time to culinary school. She was so desperately in love with this man, the chef of whom all the students were most in awe. Even though at the time she was terribly fat, she liked to believe that she was the teacher's pet, the one student he responded to as a woman, not just a cook. They were alone in the teaching kitchen and a pot simmered on the stove next to a counter filled with the ingredients for Paella. There were baskets of shellfish, bouquets of herbs, bowls of rice, tiny vessels of prized saffron.

Raul was not a tall man, but his swagger made up for his size. He spoke with a vivacious animation, his heavy Spanish accent exaggerated often, and his waxed Dali moustaches bouncing in time to his speech. He stood that day chopping, causing Angie to sigh with pleasure, the sight of him mincing garlic into oblivion, the rat-tat-tat of the knife under his steady and confident hands pure poetry in motion. He was like a great swordsman, and it made Angie swoon.

"I'll never be able to do it so fast," she sighed.

"Everything in time," Raul lisped. She jumped as he reached toward her, running his fingers under her nose. "Smell the garlic. Perfume. So beautiful," he said.

Angie's eyes watered, so she closed them, the pungent garlic wafting from his fingers into her nostrils. Raul drew a piece of basil across her lips, tickling her, and causing her to smile and open her eyes. Grabbing an unopened clam from a steamer basket, Raul held it up.

"Look at this, my little Crème Caramel. What do I have here?"

As though being quizzed in class, Angie opened her mouth to answer but Raul touched her lips with his finger, saying, "No, don't speak. I know what it is. It is a rock, nothing more. Cold as a stone. But in the hands of a man—a man with a tool—a very excellent tool—it can be opened, opened, yes, and savored." Grasping a shellfish knife, Raul began to wedge it into the clam's hinge, but he turned to look deeply into Angie's eyes, and in a foppish gesture of seduction, he raised his shoulders toward his ears, closed his eyes, and blew Angie a kiss, then screamed as though he were being carried out to sea by a man eating shark.

His accent almost impenetrable, he shrieked, "It is unthinkable! I have cut my finger. My knife is dull. I have a dull knife. Can I truly be a man with a dull knife?"

Angie grabbed a towel, and gently wrapped his hand in it, holding it tenderly, although the laceration had produced a virtually imperceptible quantity of blood.

"You're a great man. Nobody is better than you with chiles."

Comforted, Raul nodded, clicking his heels together and saying, "Yes, true! And I will set you on fire like a roasted jalapeno." Reaching for the sprig of basil he'd previously flung on the counter, he pressed it between his teeth as though it were a rose, and lurched into an arrhythmic flamenco, whisking the towel off his hand and snapping it at Angie, who watched it all wide eyed and silent.

With a gesture that far exceeded grand, Raul swept the ingredients off the counter, pressing Angie against it, kissing her passionately. She was dazzled. This great man did like—perhaps love—her. Oh, she thought, oh, yes, I am his pet. Closing her eyes and sinking into a sensation of deep bliss, Angie stood there lost in the moment and wanting it never to end.

Raul spoke. "Wait my darling."

Angie's eyes snapped open. Oh no. He was coming to his senses. He was going to send her home. But no—he didn't—he just reached over to turn off the burner.

And then they were lying on the counter, heaving and moaning against each other. As Raul began to untie her apron and remove her clothes, he muttered, barely able to speak because his words were interspersed with heaving and panting. "You are so beautiful," he gasped, "You are like the tiny threads of saffron, begging to be warmed. Like the most exotic Tahitian vanilla, and I will open your pod, liberate your sweet aromas."

But before pretty much anything could be liberated, they were greeted by a group of astonished students, who didn't dare enter the room but couldn't manage to look away. Their clothes flung on the floor, Angie and Raul each grabbed a chef's toque and attempted to regain their modesty while the students laughed and Raul snarled, "Get out of here, you mangy dishwashers," except he said it in Spanish so nobody understood or obeyed.

Angie snapped out of her reverie and turned to Ben, "Okay yes that was humiliating."

"And he was just a stand in for…" asked Ben.

"Gordon Ramsay?" laughed Angie. "C'mon they're ready for us." Ben followed Angie to the pedicure station and winced as the girl tickled his feet.

"Just hold on and bear down," said Angie.

"I'm not giving birth," he snapped, shivering a little and pulling his feet away from the determined woman who kept reaching for them. "I can't believe you go through this rigamarole every week just to see a doctor."

Angie sighed. "I really think Dr. Flicker — Kevin — has a thing for me. So please stop implying it's some wacky infatuation. I know what I'm doing this time. It's real. I'm not a kid in school any more. And I need you to believe in me."

Ben shook his head sadly. "I've believed in you since we met in third grade. I just want to protect you. To...." Ben blushed and stopped speaking as Angie smiled at him.

"You can be my best man — er...."

They both leaned back in their chairs as green masques were applied to their faces and then Ben watched Angie follow a woman into a closed room marked *Waxing*. When she yelped loudly from inside, he crossed his legs and grimaced.

Chrissy loved the way her feet felt as they skimmed across the sidewalks. She was in the Zone. The whole Zone idea didn't make much sense to her, but wherever it was, she was in it. She could run for a very long time and the more she ran, the farther she felt like running. Her breath came in even strokes and her heart pumped perfectly. She'd gone an extra mile and didn't even feel the strain. She could run, relax and look at the scenery. There were nothing but beautiful houses here, perfectly maintained landscapes to become the backdrops for all the people who lived inside these elegant, very expensive homes. And now she was one of them. It was such a far cry from when she was a nothing little sales girl at

Godiva — merely thinking the name made her shudder inside. All that de... she couldn't even think the word let alone say it. But Bill had come along like Sir Galahad and had rescued her and now here she was, living the life she had always wanted.

She ran smoothly to his — her — front door and opened it, and maximizing on endorphins, ran right into what used to be a tastefully appointed family room. The soft blue and taupe hues were very welcoming. The cottage style cushy sofa and chairs faced a big flat screen television, tastefully hidden inside an armoire crafted of reclaimed wood. Artistically painted and distressed tables sat before and beside the couch. It was at once elegant and comfortable, a place where a family could feel at home and not worry about making a mess yet which could host visitors who would look around and nod approvingly.

And now, it was her gym. She had managed to fit all the exercise equipment she wanted right into the den. The family could work out together. They didn't, but they could. She was the wife — well the girlfriend — of a Beverly Hills doctor and that required she look the part. She dug in her purse, quickly downed two over the counter diet pills as well as two special Chinese herbal pills, thinking if only she had the real thing, the thing that would make all the difference. Doubling her dosage on these pills was barely doing the job, but at least she wasn't a victim to all those old cravings. She just wasn't thinner.

Not wanting to lose any momentum, Chrissy grabbed her boxing gloves and stuffed her hands inside. Whack, whack, whack. She began socking the punching bag in the corner. Dancing and lurching and whacking. A kick. Another kick. She loved the feel of it. When people said she worked out like a cheetah on acid, she took it as a compliment. Exercise made it so much easier to stay on her diet. But she hadn't lost so much as a pound in several weeks — how was that even possible? Her plan was to investigate something called negative calorie foods although that seemed like a big lie to Chrissy. Since when did eating make calories disappear? Wait, it must be really disgusting food, the kind that made you throw up without having to stick your finger down your throat. Of course. Chrissy puzzled over this for a while, the music from her iPod rather loud, so loud in fact that she didn't hear the phone ringing.

Bill sat in his office, having cleared away the crowd of patients in his waiting room and ready for a little lunch break. His desk was like Kevin's although it contained none of the desk toys Kevin loved. Seeing those balls crash into each other and bounce back would drive Bill crazy. And he had no desire for a teeny golf game or a Zen garden either.

Thinking about the incident this morning and Candy's comments, he felt disturbed and was flipping through the photo archive on his laptop. There were many pictures of him with Chrissy and the kids. They were walking and laughing and playing and there she was, this pretty girl with red hair in a pixie cut. Her smile was bright and so endearing. There she was with Candy beside her, reading a book. There she was with Will, building something out of Legos. And then he played a video they'd made at the beach one day.

They were all seated on a blanket eating sandwiches and enjoying the day. There Bill was, so strange always to see himself, not bad he always thought, but he knew it was better than that, even if he was on the wrong side of forty, his hair gray, ok prematurely gray, but only at the sides, and his face still angular and nicely chiseled. What a catch, he thought, laughing briefly, then again the kids were moving and laughing and Chrissy was talking with them and unwrapping more sandwiches and some carrot sticks, and everyone was having a lovely time. That was the day he'd asked her to move in with them, more than a year ago. They were all so happy and it all seemed as though life was back on track.

Bill had to believe that things would be all right, that despite her current odd behavior, Chrissy was who she'd seemed to be when first they met, the girl who fit right in as part of the family. Maybe she just needed something, more assurance or something he could provide, and he would provide it. But today he'd have to discuss the Slimfast with Chrissy, so he dialed his home number. He would make the kids breakfast from now on. And either give them money or make their lunches, which he should have been doing all along. Was she still running? While listening to the phone repeatedly ring, he removed a partially eaten candy bar from his desk drawer and nibbled discretely on it.

Chrissy tried to yank the gloves off her hands but somehow they seemed to be stuck. She grabbed the phone and tried to push the button but she couldn't manage it with the gloves on. Finally she held the phone to her lips and pressed the green button with her tongue.

"Hello?" she said hastily, sounding out of breath and frustrated. She listened to what Bill was saying with a baffled look on her face. "I don't see why — what could be more nutritious?" She kept fumbling and yanking on her gloves and finally got them off with a grimace and a shrug. Reaching for the remote, she set the TV on mute, and turned on her kickboxing DVD so she could continue while talking to Bill.

"Okay, okay," she said, "Of course I know they're children. What else would they be? Midgets?" Then sighing complacently, she said, "You win. No more Slimfast. Coming home on time tonight?"

Bill casually fiddled with the candy bar wrapper, which he had folded into a ring and was trying on his left hand. "I have that game tonight with Will, remember? Why don't you and Candy come to cheer us on? We can go out for dinner after. It'll be fun."

"Eat out?" she asked, sounding as though he'd said something remarkably cruel. Chrissy amped up her kicks to match and exceed those of the group working out on the DVD. "So what about the Koush Koush?" she asked.

Bill shook his head as a resigned look crossed his face — they'd had this conversation too many times before. "The FDA is never going to approve that drug, hon, I told you. Besides it's only for the most severely overweight."

Kicking and lurching even more deeply, Chrissy was adamant, "I need it."

Bill swirled around in his chair, gazing helplessly out the window but there was nothing distracting enough to claim his attention. "Horses died on that drug during trials in India."

Chrissy scowled. She just had to let him know she was determined, make him understand that she was doing all this for him. What was wrong with Bill, anyway? He should want her to have it, not be there like some giant road block in her way. "I'm aiming for zero body fat. I can't do it without Koush Koush."

"Starvation victims have more body fat than that."

Chrissy stopped kicking and lurching briefly as she considered what he was saying. Her voice grew mournful and she sounded almost terrified. "Oh God, could you imagine that—what if you died and still had cravings—and no body." She held the phone out away from her and looked down at herself, then resumed talking. "No mouth."

Bill patiently attempted to provide assurance although inside the frustration mounted, "Now stop worrying—I mean it. Since you've been on this diet, you haven't been yourself—I'm starting to worry about you. You don't need...."

Chrissy looked up to see Will walking into the den, eyeing her suspiciously and changing the TV to one of his shows. "I'll go to India to get it if I have to. Oh—Wally's here."

Bill shook his head again. "Hon it's Will not Wally. It hurts their feelings when you get their names wrong after all this time. Listen—a diet drug out of India is not something you should mess with. Have you been taking any diet meds I don't know about?" Opening the center drawer of his desk, he removed a picture of JoEllen and gazed at it lovingly.

Will glanced toward Chrissy and precociously gave her the sort of look of disgust most teens display often and said scornfully, "You mean WILL! William Masters JUNIOR, remember?"

Kevin had been having an excellent day. Now, taking a little break, he sat at his desk as Nurse Caryn bent over the stack of journals on the floor in his office. Bill was a fool keeping all his periodicals on a shelf. He waited long enough and then slunk over to where she was standing, and spooning himself behind her, he squeezed her breasts, causing her to giggle. What a great woman. She was the perfect woman, the perfect nurse and Kevin was happy she was there when he needed to let off some steam. Envisioning another quickie in the closet, he almost didn't hear the movement by the door. When Bill entered, they jumped quickly apart and he was fairly sure Bill, who was pretty much a zombie these days, didn't catch on. Caryn exited the office with a sweet little wink in his direction as Bill slumped down in the chair in front of his desk.

"You think maybe I could ask Laura to help me plan a party for Chrissy's birthday? She's not exactly Chrissy's fan."

Hmm. This was something Kevin didn't know. "She isn't?" he asked.

"Don't you ever stop to talk to your wife any more?"

Kevin laughed. "Not if I see her coming first."

"Well, I guess it wouldn't hurt to ask her. Chrissy's going through something and I figure a party might be a nice surprise for her, show her we care."

Kevin shrugged. Why not, he thought.

Bill rose and turned to leave the office but then turned back again. "Better lay off the nurses and especially the patients. Our insurance is high enough already without sexual harassment claims."

Kevin grimaced. Maybe Bill wasn't as much of a zombie as he'd thought. "That would never happen," he said, summoning as much confidence as his voice could project. He watched as Bill just looked at him silently. And waited for Bill to leave but Bill didn't move, so he said placatingly, "Again."

"I'll call her now," said Bill.

"Really? Really?" asked Ben uncomfortably as Angie pulled him into Victoria's Secret and began showing him bras as he alternately blushed and looked for a mirror to examine the blond streaks in his already sandy hair. She held up a bra so minimal it surely wasn't meant to encapsulate adult breasts, but what Ben knew about lingerie was about equal to what he knew about female anatomy.

"Ohh," she cooed, strangely excited, "Look at this one...."

Ben looked, glanced around to see if anyone spied him looking, looked down at his shoes, then went on talking. "I just don't see it that way. He's just another old, married guy isn't he? You've never even gone on a date with him, have you?"

"I'm not buying this underwear to strain spaghetti, am I? It's coming, you'll see. This is just not like one of those incidents you keep reminding me of. I'm a grown up now, a woman, not some kid with a crush on the guy she babysits for."

"But Angie, don't you get it, it's just another version of the same thing. Remember that creepy guy with that weird kid...."

Angie remembered only too well, but she was fifteen then, and that was a long time ago. Justin's dad was the cutest guy, sort of geeky but cute and he always had that baseball cap on, even in the house. Gee, maybe he was balding? She never thought of that before. Anyway he was cute, and even though she was significantly overweight it was clear he thought she was special. They always stopped to talk as he dropped her off at her dad's after babysitting.

Eventually it escalated and one night he actually kissed her. They both moaned at the same time. "Oh Mr. Robinson," Angie had sighed.

"Angie," he yelped, his voice muffled and his lips still pressed to hers, "Ow ow ow." He sounded so orgasmic. That was what she did to him — how thrilling.

Wanting to enjoy the moment, Angie sighed, but then she jumped and Mr. Robinson yelped once more as a scary police officer rapped on the window of the car. She leaned away and Mr. Robinson wailed. Finally she wrenched her mouth away from his, as he grabbed his pinched lip, bloodied from having been caught on her braces.

The police officer had a scornful look on his face, causing Angie to blush. "Everything all right in here?" he asked, looking at Mr. Robinson as though he might actually take him into the police station. Wouldn't that be just horrible? She'd have to spend all her babysitting savings to bail him out.

Then, just to make things even worse, Angie's dad turned on the lights and looked out the door. "What's going on here? Angie, is that you?"

The police officer seemed to know her dad and waved, saying, "Don't worry, Judge, I have it under control."

Angie's dad waved and yelled, "Thanks, Frank. Send her in."

Angie had no choice then but to exit the car and trudge back toward the house. Her father had already gone back inside but it still felt humiliating. She turned toward Mr. Robinson, trying to show him some support, but he was busy with the cop, handing over his driver's license and all.

What was wrong with Ben, anyway? He had this nervy talent for making her remember stuff nobody would want to recall. What was the point anyway? Why did he have so little faith in her? He was always saying that her choices were mistakes. Didn't she have enough people in her life to do that already?

Ben knew by the expression on her face precisely what she was thinking. If only she had a clue about what was on his mind, but no, as she had been since the third grade, Angie was oblivious. He stood there then, loitering outside the dressing room, discretely looking at all the frilly stuff, wondering if ever Angie would buy that stuff for him to enjoy, when she opened the dressing room door and flashed him the bra she'd been trying on. He could see it only for a moment and then his glasses got a little steamy. Was there no air conditioning in this blasted place? Were they trying to replicate the Victorian lack of modern devices? What the devil anyway. Victoria never had stuff like this. This whole day had gone to hell. Why did he let Angie drag him to all these places? He wasn't Paris Hilton's Chihuahua so why did he let her treat him like that? He felt relieved that her doctor's appointment was imminent and he could soon flee.

Dr. Kevin Flicker liked his little projects. Always vaguely bored and disenchanted with the status quo of his daily life, Kevin regularly had one or two going simultaneously. It was what kept life interesting for him and held at bay the encroaching idea that his best years were possibly behind him. At the moment, Chrissy was his number one project. They talked on the phone nearly every day, sometimes more than once—it was titillating. There was nothing like finding a woman's soft spot and pressing it repeatedly until....

"Koush Koush?" he asked her.

Her voice was filled with the sort of beguiling desperation he most adored in a woman. "I have to have it."

Chrissy was by this time doing Yoga, and as she talked into the Bluetooth headset, she was free to move into the various poses that were so beneficial for limberness and peace of mind. At least she had achieved the limber part. She lay on her back, hips raised, repeatedly touching knee to shoulder, knee to shoulder, alternating sides.

"I could stop by the Moroccan restaurant and bring you some. With lamb or beef?" Kevin asked smoothly.

Chrissy had dropped both knees down to her shoulders and she lay in a contented little ball. "Silly," she said.

Kevin's voice grew more heated. He stroked two of the dangling balls in his Newton's Cradle desk toy,

28

weighing them in his hand. "It's gonna happen for us, you know. It's gonna be so hot, so sweet."

Still on her back, Chrissy's legs were extended straight up in the air and she opened them widely, then closed them tightly, only to open them yet again. Her breath remained steady but her voice had an odd rasp to it. "Sweet?" she asked expectantly.

Kevin smiled. He'd found the soft spot. "Yes, I'm going to start with hot fudge. And raspberries." He paused for effect, long enough for her to gain a mental picture, something he anticipated might take a few seconds, considering all. Then he said, "Have you ever really looked at my tongue?"

Chrissy was on her feet, bending over, reaching down to her toes. She hung there in the air a long while, her backside way above her head. "No," she said sincerely, "Marshmallows."

"Ooh," cooed Kevin, "Those little marshmallows that I can.... And nuts. Almonds, like...." The silver balls clanked in his hand until he jumped at the sound and let up the pressure a bit.

Chrissy stood serenely, her palms raised as if in prayer and she pressed them gently and then harder, flexing her Pecs repeatedly. She quickly interrupted him and said, "No, rich nuts, like Macadamias."

Kevin smiled, his voice seductive yet coyly amused. "Yes, Macadamias, nibbled out of...."

Chrissy had climbed up onto the Stairmaster and was frenetically stepping up and down, up and down, up and down. Her pace was frenzied despite all the Yoga, and she looked flushed and agitated. Marching even more swiftly, she said, "And whipped cream, blasting out of the can."

Kevin closed his eyes briefly, then said, "Have you ever seen my...."

Chrissy's breath was raspy, her heart thundering. She touched her wrist and then with eyes wide with shock, dropped her arm as though she'd burned herself. Her eyes bulged — her pulse was racing — this wasn't good, not good at all — her heart rate was the one thing she counted on to be ever steady. She jumped off the Stairmaster and began doing Yoga again, raising her arms high overhead, touching palms together and bringing them down straight in front of her body, touching her belly button, then gracefully separating her palms and fluttering her arms out to the sides to make a big circle back to the top of her head where her palms once again met. She focused on her breathing, attempting to normalize her heart rate.

"You have to stop doing this to me, Kevin. I'm serious. We can talk about..." she paused for a long moment, her eyes getting glassy, and then she said, "Fudge...." And she paused once more, coming into focus again and continued, "But you know Bill is my rock. He's not a player like you. He'd never cheat on me. I'd go crazy if he did, I'd...."

Kevin laughed. He had her. It was just a matter of time. "Oh c'mon. Bill is no saint. He's just never been improperly tempted...." Kevin laughed again, lowered his voice to its most seductive register, then said, "We didn't even get to salty."

Chrissy was down on her knees, raising her hands over head and leaning forward, her arms stretched outward as her body folded down over her knees and out against the floor. "Salty," she repeated, tantalized by the thought.

Kevin started raking his little sand pit, making swirl after swirl in the sand with the tiny rake. "I could pack you in popcorn....Eat my way in."

Chrissy sat flat on the floor, her legs open widely. Arms behind her head, she leaned first left then right, touching elbow to knee and up again. "No," she said adamantly. "Chips."

At last. They were together at last. Angie sat on the examining table, attempting to make her paper gown seem as seductive as possible. Ignoring Nurse Leona, who stood silently in the corner of the room like one of those eunuchs who guarded the harem, Angie shrugged her shoulder subtly, but gazing into Dr. Flicker's eyes as she did it, allowing the gown to slip down a bit so he could have an eyeful of the sexy bra she'd just bought.

Glancing at his nurse, Kevin casually lifted the gown back up onto her shoulder and patted her paternally on the back. "Okay, you can dress now and meet me in my office," he said.

Angie loved the tête-à-têtes they had weekly. She sat in the chair facing him, perched on the edge so she could lean as much toward him as possible. He was so magnetic, how could she avoid it. She'd deliberately left the two top buttons on her sweater undone and leaning forward just made her cleavage pop even more.

She reached for the little cue stick off the tiny pool table on top of his desk and stroked it seductively with her finger, the bright polish on her nails twinkling in the light. This was going so well. It would happen soon, she just knew it—her life was about to begin.

Dr. Flicker looked up from her chart and smiled at Angie, causing her to beam at him in return. "You've done just great. Not a single backslide, even another pound gone since last week. I wish all my patients were just like you."

Angie leaned forward even more, although it began to feel a little precarious on the edge of the chair. She said, "I just decided to trust my instincts. Never taste anything. Just cook."

Dr. Flicker looked up and seemed quite perplexed. "Aren't you a caterer? Can you really do that? Must be hard."

Angie flirtatiously lowered her chin and raised her eyes, gazing coyly at Kevin. "I like hard things," she said, smiling. "Come back with me to my restaurant. I'll make you a fabulous lunch." She gazed into his eyes, attempting to ignite a fire in him to match what she was feeling. "Your tongue will thank you."

"Your blouse is unbuttoned," he said with what she was certain was veiled passion.

Angie leaned in even further. Closer and closer she wanted to get but the giant desk was in the way. Her breast was brushing against those dangling balls, causing them to clank. But look—he was leaning in too. It was working! Angie rose, moving swiftly toward Kevin, who reached for her.

And then another doctor leaned in the room and Angie had to snap back to attention and so did Kevin. What horrid luck.

"I'm taking your wife to lunch," Bill said.

"Glad somebody's taking her," said Kevin in a way that made Angie certain he would soon be bound for the divorce courts. But why had Dr. Flicker resumed sitting behind the giant desk? It was like a barricade between them.

When the other doctor had gone, Angie tried to recapture the moment. She said softly, "Come to my deli for lunch."

As Kevin rose and walked around the desk, Angie's heart nearly stopped beating. He reached for her and took her hand, rather gently she thought — how sweet. But then he said, "What sort of doctor would I be...."

Oh no! Everything was devolving, swirling into a curdling mass of goo. But she wouldn't, couldn't let it. She had to regain the moment, recapture his ardor, which Angie knew simmered there below the surface. Maybe he just didn't realize how strong it was. "I know you feel it, Dr. Flicker," she said, pausing, then, more intimately, "Kevin."

He smiled at her in a kindly way which she took as a horrible sign. "You're a beautiful girl," he said, "What man wouldn't want you? Who could blame me? If not for this, I'd grab you and never let go."

Kevin had extended his naked left hand toward Angie, who regarded it and looked up at him quizzically. Determinedly he pointed toward his ringless ring finger. "This," he said adamantly.

Lowering her voice a bit, Angie purred, "I could be your mid-life crisis."

Smiling deeply at Angie, Kevin rose to his feet. Angie was groping inside her purse and finally extracted a business card. Reaching forward seductively while trying to avoid setting those dangling balls aclatter, Angie grabbed a pen from his desk and scribbled on the back of the card. "Work number on front, home on back. Any time Kevin, day or night. I mean it."

Swaggering noticeably, Kevin walked Angie out the door of his office. What a great day. Maybe he could take a bite out of this little cupcake one day. Why not? She was begging for it and how could he be so cruel as to deny her?

TWO

Bill enjoyed the smooth ride his Mercedes provided and he thought of little on his way to meet Laura at a popular lunch place where he could have a good meal with no recriminations. Eating at home had become unpleasant, something else he should deal with but didn't have the heart to confront.

Most of the major east-west boulevards now were littered with a collection of electronic billboards like giant televisions, and there to his left was a rather spectacular anti-smoking billboard that he knew had come from Laura and her organization. It depicted a cemetery, and the image was so pristine, it was almost three-D. A casket sat open with a young corpse inside, and floating over the body was a human-sized lit cigarette, producing very realistic smoke. The caption said *Smoke Now, Die Later*, but the word *Later* was crossed out and above it was the word *Sooner*. Bill thought the campaign was very impressive. He also thought it wouldn't work because people who wanted to smoke didn't even respond to medical logic let alone billboards. Smokers had the strongest system of disbelief of most of the addicts he'd confronted. It was a shame.

Thinking with some degree of guilt about how little time recently he'd had to devote to the anti-smoking coalition, he almost drove right by Spago, where he was meeting Laura. Bill came to a quick stop and a valet whisked the car away while he entered Wolfgang Puck's celebrated eatery.

He stopped briefly at the desk and spoke to a host who greeted him warmly, seemed to remember and recognize him although he hadn't dined there in way too long, and courteously led him to Laura, who was already seated at one of their charming patio tables. She waved as she saw him, and she seemed to be smiling happily, so perhaps he'd been too sensitive assuming she'd been angry at him.

Laura was still radiant, a healthy looking blonde who didn't seem ever to have food issues. She had never been overweight, but was the sort of solid, relatively athletic person who could help you lift a table if necessary. How JoEllen would laugh at that description. It was Laura who had introduced them, way back in college, and they'd all remained best friends ever after. He noted she still carried everywhere that giant bag, more briefcase than purse, and he assumed her habit of handing out anti-smoking paraphernalia hadn't changed. It took a lot of nerve to do that, and Bill gave her credit for moxxy.

He touched her on the shoulder, leaned down to kiss her cheek and sat beside her in the garden. This was a lovely spot. Perhaps they could hold the party here. "Just saw one of your billboards. *Smoke now, die sooner*. Really great."

"We try to get more and more in your face with the ads. I just wish the kids would take them more seriously. They think they're immortal. I want to do a big one featuring that kid who took up chewing tobacco in high school and was dead within a year. Show close ups of what the surgery did to him, not that it did any good."

"That was a huge tragedy, but a very unusual case," Bill said.

"I don't think it was so unusual, just a bit fast. Kids need to believe it can happen to them."

Bill nodded, agreeing with everything she was saying. "Sorry I haven't had more time to work with you and the board on it. You know I want to but…"

"Chrissy," Laura said disdainfully.

Bill sighed and spoke a bit haltingly but with sincerity, "I'd hoped you'd forgiven me. It was almost a year after JoEllen died before we began dating, and she would have understood."

Laura sounded angry, but Bill couldn't see why she was still so infuriated. "Men need company, we all know that. I just couldn't see how you could replace Jo with a-a-I'm sorry, but a bimbo."

Bill nodded to the busboy who'd brought them water and a basket of beautiful breads. After he was out of earshot, Bill said, "I don't think you're being fair to her. You don't even really know her." Then he sighed with painful depth and finally continued, "I felt like hiding under the covers every day, you know that. You know what she meant to me, to us all. Finally I said, no, okay, I'm gonna live, not hide."

Laura's face softened but before she could respond a waiter had arrived to introduce himself and take their order. To his request if they wanted something from the bar, Laura replied, "Oh I think this diet soda's plenty."

Bill nodded, "Yes it's lunch, let's just eat."

"Shall I give you another minute?" asked the waiter congenially.

Bill held up one finger as they both glanced hastily at their menus. "Want to share salmon blini or a shrimp pizza to start?" Bill asked Laura, who nodded, causing him to order both.

"Maybe I'll try that lobster cobb salad," said Laura.

"Fantastic," said Bill, "I was tempted to have the lobster club but think I'll do the grilled rib eye—comes with potatoes. Not sure I remember what one is any more. Gotta get the calories and the carbs out. Not to mention fried."

Laura laughed and patted Bill's hand. "Poor starving doctor boy," she cooed.

As the waiter departed, Laura left her hand on Bill's for an extra second. "It's okay," she said, I'm not expecting you to become a monk. So—what about this party?"

"I just wanted to do something nice for Chrissy's birthday. She seems very insecure lately, as though she's going through something and the current diet has her way on edge, but I'm trying to talk her through that, so I thought maybe if I threw her a party, made her feel special, she'd calm down a little, return to being that sweet girl who charmed the kids so much at the mall when we met her."

"Leave it to you to meet a girl who gives you a free piece of Godiva and you move her into your house."

Bill laughed. "Never underestimate the power of chocolate on the human heart."

"You're right. I never trust people who're allergic to chocolate. So were you going to have the party at home or out somewhere?"

"I don't know. I never had to plan a party before. Maybe some place simple, sweet, elegant—like this patio—it's really pretty here, isn't it?"

"All right," said Laura, "I'll go home, think about it, make a few calls, come up with a list of potential places, some ideas for the menu, and we can go look at them one day next week? Maybe you could take a couple hours off toward the end of the day?"

Bill nodded. "Sounds great." He moaned softly then and said, "Oh my God, taste these blini. Why don't I come here every day? Maybe I will from now on."

"Pizza's great too," said Laura, "Wolfie never misses."

After eating their lunch and talking about old times, Bill and Laura strolled a bit, still in a relatively convivial mood and moving toward a jewelry store where Bill could ask Laura's advice about some sort of present for Chrissy. They approached a gym called Zero Tolerance, but before they could continue, Laura spotted a young couple on the sidewalk smoking. She signaled wait to Bill, dug into her bag and smoothly removed the flyers she intended to pass along, hoping to convert them on the spot.

Laura's voice was impassioned but gentle, but the urgency with which she spoke caused the couple to react to her with some level of discomfort, probably unrelated to the subject of her tirade. "The choices you make now are so important, so long lasting," she said maturely but kindly. "You can't even imagine how you'll feel twenty years from now about something you're doing today. Maybe you won't want it at all, but by then you'll be stuck with it. It'll be a habit, a bad habit, but one you might not have the courage to break."

Bill listened silently as Laura continued her harangue and he wondered was she talking completely about smoking or was something more personal under the surface working its way up.

"Think about it," she implored, "Now is the time to break those nasty habits, not to get sucked in too deeply into something you'll regret later on. *Please!* Give it some thought. Here, take this. Take two. It's not too late to change now. You can do it. You really can."

Silently the young couple each accepted the flyers and nodded to Laura wordlessly then turned to walk off in the other direction. Bill put a kindly hand on Laura's arm and together they walked forward. He glanced back, noting that the kids had tossed the flyers in the nearest trash can. Shaking his head, he refocused on what Laura was now saying.

"You know," she said wistfully, "Last night I dreamed George came back. I didn't even tell Kevin about it. You know how he felt. Such a competition."

Bill nodded. Kevin was quite insane on the subject of George.

"You remember it all, right?" asked Laura, murmuring softly, "George and me, walking along, and out of nowhere that jerk, and he swerved and I pulled on George, but he didn't move fast enough." Suddenly she began to weep, very intensely Bill thought, considering how long it had been, and he faced her, his hand on her arm, stroking it softly.

"He was reaching for a cigarette, did you know that?" she asked, "That's why he didn't see us."

Her tears grew stronger and Bill just wrapped his arms around her, hoping it would help and she would feel a little better. He patted her kindly on the back.

"I didn't know that last part, no," he said.

Despite having pretty much every workout gadget any girl could ever want right there at home in the den, Chrissy often liked to vary her days and that usually meant a trip to her favorite spot, a super high tech gym called Zero Tolerance. It gave her energy to work out alongside other motivated people and if she wanted to talk, there was always someone to chat up on the treadmills. At this moment, she'd finished a workout, had showered, and was carrying her gym bag as she walked toward the parking garage nearby. Just as she was about to cross the street, she noticed something shocking. There in the middle of the sidewalk was her Bill, embracing Kevin's Laura — right out in public.

She gasped audibly and then with much astonishment, clapped her hand over her mouth, as though her gasps could cause her to be noticed when she wasn't the one committing a flagrant act of infidelity, right there on the sidewalk. She stood frozen for a while, for as long as their nauseating embrace continued, but then as they began walking, so did she.

Like a character in a movie trying to outsmart a sniper, she serpentined along, darting into doorways, sidling around corners, expecting at any moment that Bill would turn around and spot her. Quick thinking — that was what she needed. Reaching into her gym bag, she extracted her hoodie and tied it around her head with the arms linked under her chin. That would surely provide some cover. Unconcerned that she looked a bit like someone from the old country about to exit Ellis Island, Chrissy was determined to follow them.

They walked half a block or so and she continued her covert stalking. Were they going to a hotel? What would they think when she burst into the room, after a suitable pause of course. She would catch them in the act and then who would have the power? But no, they entered a small jewelry store, one with very beautiful pieces in the window, and that only made Chrissy sadder. Lurking outside the store, she tried to see all without being seen. If only she could hear, but no, not a word. But hey, a picture was worth a thousand cheaters, wasn't it? As she saw what came next, her stomach dropped and she thought she'd lose it all, right there in the street. Bill had fastened a diamond necklace on Laura, who held up her hair and looked in the mirror.

Chrissy raised her hands, shaking them back and forth as though she were at some peculiar religious revival meeting. "Oh, Oh, Oh," she mumbled again and again. She pulled her cell phone out of her pocket and slowly punched in the numbers as she whispered each one, something she did every time she made this call. "What's the damn number? Oh crap. 1-800-what-wait—oh 1-800-s-h-r-i-n-k. Wait that's not enough numbers. What's the last one? Every freaking time. Another K? s-h-r-i-n-k-*k*? No wait, that's not it, that's the racist group. Oh crap and double crap. Wait, wait, hmmm, maybe…." Finally she remembered, and triumphantly dialed 1-800-s-h-r-i-n-k-U." It rang several times but at last Ben picked up the phone. Thank goodness.

"Yes," she said, "It's Chrissy." She took a deep breath as he was speaking, then answered quickly, "Very upset." With each pause her shrink said something to which she would respond. "Bill, cheating on me with his partner's wife." Ben was talking then and she waited politely, only half hearing what he was saying, then she continued, "She was in his arms, that's proof, isn't it? I saw them."

Bill and Laura had by this time exited the jewelry store but carried no packages. Spotting them, Chrissy quickly turned her back, angling her face into a wall. Momentarily Bill noticed her, looked quizzically, then shook his head dismissively and continued walking with Laura who was asking him a question.

"Just how serious are you about this girl?"

Bill shrugged.

"Once you start buying diamonds, there's really only one direction in which to go. Is that where you really want to go? Can you see yourself with her ten years down the road?"

"I could see myself with JoEllen until the end of time," he replied. "Look how reliably that worked out."

"I'm just saying that maybe a nice gift, but a less diamond-specific one might be a better choice."

"I know she wants an exercise room. I could have the guest house converted into a gym instead I guess. Or do that and get her a bracelet. A bracelet isn't that promise of foreverish is it?"

"No," said Laura, "Maybe not. I just really wonder why you feel compelled to do all this. I think there's more happening here that maybe you don't realize."

"First you fatten me up at lunch and now you want to shrink me?" Bill joked.

Ben was busy on the computer, typing to one of his therapy clients. He had just a few left who insisted on doing therapy via instant message, mostly the super shy ones who were afraid of having their voices heard, but he didn't mind. Helping people was helping people. His day had improved after he parted with Angie and let her go on to her doctor's visit. There was always someone who needed his wisdom and if the one person he wanted most to help refused to comprehend what he was saying, there was always tomorrow.

Just as he signed off with Rex, a gay agoraphobic who felt guilty for hiring call boys and then not letting them into his apartment, Ben's roommate Clint arrived with a pizza and a six-pack of beer. Clint was the quintessential California boy, ripped, chiseled, gorgeous, and basically a congenial narcissist.

It didn't take overly long for Clint to notice Ben's hair and comment, "Woah. Cool."

Ben grunted in a miserable way, saying, "I jump every time I look in the mirror."

"No worries, dude, you're totally cool. Took guts for you to do that."

Ben flopped on the couch and shoved a slice of pizza in his mouth, speaking clumsily. "I did it for Angie, but she still doesn't know I'm alive. It's like she thinks we're girlfriends."   He sat chewing silently, pondering this untenable situation and then asked, "What would you do, Clint? I mean if a girl didn't notice you?"

The horror of such an improbability struck Clint deeply. "Whoa! Say what?"

Ben answered earnestly, as though such a possibly could actually exist. "You know—you like a girl but she doesn't notice you."

"You mean like she's a lesbian?" asked Clint, sincerely.

Ben shook his head, his mouth stuffed with pizza. "No," he said emphatically, "Just doesn't notice you."

Clint was incredulous. "And like she doesn't come up to me and give me her number? Dude! That's heavy."

"I just have to make Angie see that I'm better for her than that old fart." He popped open a can of beer and took a deep swig. "Right now for all I know, she thinks I'm gay."

Clint laughed. "So tell her you're straight. Show her your macho side, they love that. Let her watch you work out. No, you don't work out." Then it was as though the light had dawned and Clint had experienced some sort of religious conversion. "Dude! You gotta work out more. Later tonight, you and me, shoot some hoops."

Ben hunched his shoulders and shrugged. He knew hoops wasn't the answer but what was the point of continuing. It would be like asking Julia Child how to deal with people who never wanted to eat.

At the same moment, Angie was exiting her car and about to enter the guest house behind her dad's home where she'd lived since she was old enough to have her own place. Filled with excitement about her interaction with Kevin, she hummed a little tune and felt glad to be alive. When she noticed her dad outside watering his lawn, she waved excitedly.

"Hi Daddy!" she said with happiness and enthusiasm. "Brought you some just-invented gelato — olive-praline." She smiled at her dad and walked toward him, balancing the containers adroitly.

Judge, whose crotchety demeanor made him seem far older than his fifty-two years, considered himself a nice guy who'd just been in a very bad mood for while, waved dismissively at his daughter. Olive ice cream? What the blazes was she talking about? "You're making footprints on the wet lawn," he said, a touch too loud.

"But I made this just for you," she said, her outlook growing stormier by the moment. Filled with the courage generated by her meeting with Dr. Flicker, she pressed on, sidestepping the stream of water adroitly and almost managing to place a kiss on her dad's cheek.

He said, "Watch it, there's water here." And he stepped back a few feet.

She kept trying. "Have you had dinner yet? I could make you something."

He frowned. "I can't eat that wacky stuff you make. You know that. Don't worry I can microwave something once the lawn is done. You enjoy your evening."

Totally deflated, Angie walked away, turning back once to say, "And you don't want your special ice cream? It's Italian."

He shook his head and waved dismissively, without even seeing the fallen look on her face, and turned to water the side of the house.

Angie walked to her own doorway, turned the key in the lock and stepped inside, sad and seething. It was always like this — why did she expect anything more? She looked down at the containers she carried as though they held gelato flavored with arsenic. Or maybe she wished they did.

Candy was equally livid as she entered her front door, slamming it so loudly neighbors half a block away could hear. Chrissy approached her looking puzzled and not just a little irritated.

Candy's tone was accusatory, "You forgot to pick me up again! I had to call Aunt Laura."

Chrissy registered genuine shock and remorse, and removing the cold cloth with which she had swaddled her forehead, she said "Oh my God! I'm so sorry, Cindy."

Candy grew instantly more enraged. "My name isn't Cindy — it's CANDY — Candy — didn't they teach you that word when you worked at the mall — in a God damn candy shop?" Candy's eyes opened wide. She'd never said those words before. Good thing Daddy wasn't here to hear her. Or her teacher. Or Will. Will would be sure to tell on her and who knew what the punishment was for saying that. But she was glad she said the words and she thought them again. God damn. God damn Chrissy.

Holding her head with one hand, and looking as though the only thing preventing her brains from exploding out one side was the pressure she was applying,

Chrissy walked over closer to Candy, put her arm around the child, attempting to call a truce, but by the expression on her face it was clear she wasn't really focused on her sin du jour. Maybe the little girl would understand if she explained.

"I just had a really really really terrible day," Chrissy said. "Okay?" She peered into Candy's eyes, looking for signs of absolution, signs which were not forthcoming. "You can see I'm stressed, can't you?" Candy was unyielding. Chrissy realized this could become a serious problem, so she decided to offer the child a consolation. "Be good and we can have a special girls' dinner together later, okay? You can dress up if you want to and we can even look at your sticker book."

Candy peered suspiciously at Chrissy. She didn't trust the offer that had just been tendered, but she did like looking at her sticker book. "What should I wear?" she asked.

"Whatever you want, of course," said Chrissy, smiling through a grimace that was designed to generate sympathy for her and her really really really bad day. "You go get dressed up and I'll set the table, okay?"

Candy nodded and went off to her room, where she pulled an old princess Halloween costume from her dress up trunk along with a feather boa and several strands of plastic pearls, cheering up a little as she draped them around her neck. But where was her crown? She looked and looked but it wasn't in the dress up trunk. She did have a magic wand, though, so maybe that would do. She looked in the mirror. Maybe it all would work out okay. Maybe she would have fun with Chrissy and it would be like it was when they first met and she laughed and played with them and brought them little gold boxes of chocolate.

Candy walked into the dining room and curtseyed and it seemed as though Chrissy were smiling, in a genuine way. Look—there were crystal glasses on the table—the kind grownups used for wine—this was exciting—Candy wasn't normally allowed to have wine or to touch those glasses. She saw they contained only water with a lemon slice on the side, but still it would be fun to feel like a grown up and drink from them.

Candy sat at her place at the table and watched expectantly as Chrissy walked into the dining room carrying a huge silver platter with a giant silver dome on it. Had she made a turkey? Candy didn't smell anything.

With a flourish, Chrissy set the tray on the table and removed the dome, revealing four rice cakes, some carrot curls, four celery sticks, a couple lettuce wedges, and some lemon halves. She'd put a small bowl of salad dressing next to the lettuce and beside it was a dropper, just like Daddy used to give Candy medicine. What?

Candy's vicious mood resumed instantly. "Are you kidding me? I'm a growing kid. I need food. I have the rest of my life to diet." She glared at Chrissy, even angrier because her tiny glimmer of hope had once again been crushed. Grabbing one of the rice cakes, she snapped it into pieces and was about to hurl it at Chrissy when she thought better of it. She'd surely be punished for that. But she looked at Chrissy furiously and tossed the broken pieces back down on the tray.

"But Cindy," said Chrissy softly.

Enraged, the child began screaming, "It's Candy. Candy. Candy. Why don't you eat a piece—your brain needs the sugar." Then she glared furiously at Chrissy and said loudly, "God damn it."

Candy got down from her chair and walked into the kitchen, where she dragged one of the chairs in there over to the counter, climbed onto it and reached into a high shelf and extracted the jar of peanut butter. She then sat in the chair, opened the jar and shoved her hand inside, licking the peanut butter off.

Candy began to weep as she licked her hand, but before she could launch into a full blown crying jag, there was a faint tap tap tap at the door leading from the dining area in the kitchen to the back yard. She ran to open the door as Chrissy entered the kitchen, also ready to see who was there.

Sophie, thought Chrissy with annoyance. Mrs. G, thought Candy, elated to see that her hands were not empty. Candy flung open the door and hurled herself into Mrs. G's arms, almost upending the tray of food she carried.

Taking one savvy look around the kitchen, Sophie entered the house and smiled. "Hello, girls, I came to beg you to do me a favor."

"Please," said Candy in an exaggeratedly adult way, "Do come in. We're always here to help." She sniffled then and most of her tears disappeared.

Sophie set the tray down on the counter and turned toward the girls. "You know my poor hubby Bert of course, right? Well he's a terrible food addict. Determined to eat all the wrong things. I'm so worried about his health. He's a geezer you know."

"I thought maybe he was a geezer," said Candy. Later she would ask Will what that was.

"I love my Bert, so when he begs me to make lasagna and strudel, what can I do? I have to do it. It would hurt his feelings if I said 'Shut up geezer, and eat your bran flakes.'" Sophie smiled at Candy as she said this.

"Nobody wants to hear that," said Candy.

"So I was wondering if you'd take this lasagna off my hands," asked Sophie. Maybe we could sit together and have a meal. Is Bill home yet?"

"Bill is off with Wally at a father-son ballgame," said Chrissy.

"*Will*," said Sophie with some emphasis, looking right at Chrissy, "Is a very nice boy. With a good appetite. So — get some plates and let's sit. I think you girls could use a talk."

Chrissy threw up her hands in submission. What was she to do? Maybe she could hide the food in a napkin and toss it later. She handed the plates to Sophie, who took them to the kitchen table, saying, "Cozier right here. We don't need to mess up the dining room."

"No," said Candy sardonically, "You don't want to see what's in there."

Sophie made three plates of food with the giant lasagna she'd brought as well as a salad and some garlic bread and watched happily as Candy began eating with enthusiasm. She looked at Chrissy, who clearly was miserable, and so she said in her usual motherly way, "Something bothering you, dear?"

Uncharacteristically, Chrissy burst into tears. "I had a big shock today," she said. "Something I never believed I'd witness, I saw. My whole world is upside down. Migraine all afternoon."

Sophie patted Chrissy's hand. "It can't be as bad as all that."

Chrissy sobbed. "All I ever wanted was to make Bill happy. For Cindy and Wally to be happy too. For us to be a family. I never had a real family of my own you know. I just want to be the beautiful wife Bill wants me to be."

Her mouth full of food, Candy spoke up. "You see what I'm dealing with?" she asked Mrs. G.

As she dried her eyes, Chrissy began gazing at the lasagna, and almost involuntarily, her hand reached out, her fork dug into the pasta and into her mouth it went. Her eyes closed and simultaneous expressions crossed her face, orgasmic pleasure and utter revulsion.

Sophie turned her attention to Candy. "Sweetheart, what a good eater you are. You did a great job with your dinner. And you stayed so neat too. Do you think it's safe to eat dessert with your princess gown on? That strudel can be drippy."

Candy smiled at Mrs. G. Then she rose from her seat and hurled herself into the old lady's arms. "If I had a gram, I'd want her to be just like you," she said sincerely.

"Ahh," sighed Sophie, thinking of her grandkids, up in the Bay Area and seldom around to see her when she visited. "I can be your honorary gram any time you want."

Candy hugged her more tightly, then said, "If you think I should change, I will," and she ran off to her room.

Sophie reached out to Chrissy and touched her hand. "Listen to me, deary. I knew Bill's wife very well. She was a happy person. She ate real food. She cooked. Sometimes she baked cookies. She planted flowers. She knew the kids' names. She lived. If you want to be the wife Bill wants, be like that. Live. Stop all this nonsense with the working out all day and dieting until your brain is addled. Be reasonable."

Chrissy looked at her as though she were being attacked.

"And you know what else about Bill's wife?" she asked while Chrissy miserably shook her head, wishing this old lady would leave already. "She looked like you. So you know what that means?"

Chrissy gazed mournfully down at her sneakers and said almost inaudibly, "Yes. That I'm a stand in. What do they call it in the movies? A stunt double."

Sophie smiled knowingly, shook her head and said, "It means you're his type."

Finally Chrissy smiled. But she knew something Sophie didn't, something that was not a hopeful sign. And as she began to whisper what she'd seen, Candy returned, wearing play clothes, so she couldn't say a word.

"Now," said Sophie, "Let's have dessert. Where's that ice cream I tucked into the freezer?"

Laura sat at the small desk in her kitchen, papers piled everywhere. She worked with total absorption, the anti-smoking campaign always at the forefront in her mind. Her hand raced across a small pad as she listed a number of ideas to explore in more detail later. There were so many folders on the small space that you could barely see the beloved picture of George, and obliterated was all but the top of the silver frame where his name was engraved. But George wasn't on her mind at the moment. She wanted to come up with a really big idea, something that would finally reach the people who were most resistent to prior campaigns.

As she flipped the page and began to fill the next with additional jottings, the ink ran out in her pen. She gave it a shake and tried again, but no, nothing. She pawed at the folders on the desk, moving everything, looking for another pen and in the process, revealing the beautiful picture of George, with his toothy grin, his strong, sharp teeth prominent in his mouth. He had been so wonderful. She gently touched the frame and smiled softly.

Then Laura rose and walked toward Kevin's den. It was his home office and he had a similar setup to what was at work, with duplicates of all the desk toys. In the room were other, larger items, a mini putting green, a mini basketball hoop. Basically it was a college dorm room but with fewer books and no pictures of pro cheerleaders or minor actresses.

Before she could enter the room she heard his voice, at a whisper, but nevertheless audible. He was talking to someone he shouldn't be. Laura knew what to expect but she stopped anyway, waiting to hear what he was saying.

"All I have to do is think of you and it happens," he whispered. Then after a pause, he continued, "No it's you. I've never wanted a woman this much."

Laura shook her head as she heard Kevin's end of the conversation and easily inserted what was being said on the other side. The only thing she didn't know was whose voice it was, but how did that matter. Some version of this conversation had been taking place for years in her marriage and the woman on the other end of the line never was Laura.

Peculiarly he said next, "I wouldn't even have to stop for the fudge. Got a jar in the car."

Fudge, thought Laura. What on earth was his game now? This was definitely a new angle.

"That game will go on for hours," insisted Kevin and then imploringly, "Let me come over."

Laura bowed her head, a sad but wry expression on her face. It never ended. Yet she never did anything about it. To her this was a personal indictment and it made her feel rotten about herself even more than about Kevin, even more than about their marriage, which clearly was long dead, just not yet buried.

Then Kevin snickered, "You kidding—she wouldn't even notice. Let me worry about my wife."

Despite her desire to be a wry sophistocate who could take this betrayal in stride because she'd already had so much practice, a look of pain crossed Laura's face. As she began to creep away she heard his last comment.

"He's not the saint you think he is."

Dirty and jubliant, Bill and Will burst through the door carrying baseball equipment and looking like they'd just come in from winning a war. "Girls!" shouted Bill, "We won! You missed a great game."

Chrissy, feeling apprehensive about Bill, tense about what might transpire that evening, and guilty about having eaten a massive three bites of lasagna, approached him tentatively. He grabbed her like a swashbuckling Errol Flynn, of whom she'd never heard, and kissed her with bravado. Not enjoying the sense that she was being toyed with, Chrissy tensed up and became even more withdrawn. Her voice cold and angry, she said, "You reek!"

Bill laughed and hugged her, oblivious to the mini drama that was playing inside her mind. "Yeah, we need showers."

Scowling ever more deeply, she said, "Of pizza."

Observing this, Will headed for his room as Bill said crossly, "For God's sake. I'm going to shower. We can talk after."

Talk! Bill had said talk. Chrissy knew what that meant — it was obvious what was coming. Her head began to pound again, not that it had ever stopped. Pacing and beginning to hyperventilate, she reached for the phone and while dialing, she bent over, placing her head between her knees. If she'd had a paper bag, she would have been breathing into it.

She performed the usual ritual in attempting to recall Ben's number, dialing 1-800-shrinkk several times before she got it correct and ultimately got the phone to ring. When Ben answered, her voice was truly mournful, "Hi, it's Chrissy again. It's over, I know it's over. He wants to talk. What am I supposed to do now?"

As Ben's voice came through at the other end of the line, she resumed pacing, hearing only part of what he was saying, politely waiting until it would be her turn again to speak. "I tell you I won't go back to Godiva. I won't! I can't! No. Never again."

Then she paused and almost considered Ben's question, to which she replied, "No, he didn't say that." And again a pause and a reply, "No, I didn't try that."

Her pacing heated up and as she listened to what was an attempt on his part to calm her down, she walked to her purse and began digging it in, but couldn't find what she sought, so she dumped the contents out and began pawing through them. There were mini exercise gadgets, empty prescription bottles, which she opened although she knew their contents were long ago used up, and just for good measure, she gave them a shake before hurling each one down. With trembling hands, she opened a lipstick, applied it without a mirror, then twitched and freaked out a bit more, shook her head, then rubbed the lipstick off on the back of her hand. Wondering was it too late to take her over the counter diet pills, she shrugged with intense frustration and downed several.

Interrupting Ben, she said, "And you're absolutely sure psychologists can't prescribe drugs?" It didn't matter how many times previously she'd asked that question, she continued as though it had never before been expressed, "But that doesn't include Valium, right?"

Bill had showered and tucked the kids in for the night and by this time was in the bed, a thick stack of medical journals on his bedside table. Instead of reading, he was holding a small, framed photo of his wife and kids. He gazed at it peacefully, now and then running his finger across the glass.

Bill spotted Chrissy entering the bedroom from their bathroom and hastily stashed the picture back in his bedside drawer as she stopped to spritz herself with some perfume.

Tense and still overwrought, it was her plan to seduce Bill, to remind him of all the things about her he loved, even though she couldn't enumerate any of them at the moment. She was wearing a beautiful peignoir set which any man would like and she knew exactly what to do. She clicked on the stereo, turning the volume low, and launched into her plan of attack.

How many evenings had she worked out on the treadmill while *Dancing with the Stars* was on television? She didn't know how many, but a lot. How many times had she seen those lithe TV dancers perform the Rhumba, the dance of love? Also a lot. So this was her chance to writhe and wriggle her way back into Bill's heart—and his pants.

Bill looked up, quite surprised to see Chrissy squirming along in the room, doing some sort of new exercise maneuver. It didn't look like Yoga exactly, but it did involve some hip thrusts and several leg kicks. This was getting serious. Now she was dressing in seductive lingerie to work out. She never stopped working out. Her movements became jerkier and jerkier and Bill began to wonder would she dislocate a hip or a shoulder. There was something that looked like a squat thrust. Terrified to keep watching, but too entranced to glance away, Bill watched with a combined expression of confusion and horror.

Finally the workout ended, and Chrissy climbed into bed without even having broken a sweat. She grabbed Bill in some sort of wrestler's hold and began kissing his neck so strenuously he began to wonder had she somehow converted to vampirism during the day. Kindly he encircled her shoulders and gave them a squeeze, hoping to calm her a bit.

"We need to talk," he said softly.

Chrissy lurched to a sitting position and gazed all about the room, clearly growing more and more frantic. "I knew it. I knew it," she said repeatedly.

"I'm worried about you," said Bill in a concerned voice that gave new meaning to the term bedside manner. "You're overdoing the diet. You're not yourself. Laura told me you forgot to pick up Candy."

Hearing that name drove Chrissy into an even deeper frenzy. She was nearly beyond words and could only say "Laura!" with a tone normally reserved for the names of traitors in cinematic thrillers.

"You're half hysterical all the time lately," said Bill.

"It's the Koush Koush," she replied, unable to devise any other line of response. "I can't believe you won't get it for me. If I were your patient, you would. What's the point of living with a doctor if he won't…."

Bill tensed and his face grew stormy. "This nonsense has got to end."

End! Chrissy had heard the word *end* and was terrified. "Okay, okay," she said, climbing on top of Bill and wriggling a bit.

Bill responded to her kisses for only a few moments, realized he didn't have the energy for anything more, then gently maneuvered her off of him. "Honey, I'm just too beat. I got up at six. Here, c'mere." Thinking they could snuggle down beneath the covers and drift off peacefully to sleep, Bill turned off the light and took Chrissy in his arms.

She lay there, wide awake and clenched within his embrace, her heart pounding with stress, her face worried and suspicious, but of course by then he was asleep.

THREE

Kevin observed with some small degree of scorn Bill busily scribbling notes on a collection of patients' charts. He was always such a boy scout. "Hey, buddy!" said Kevin, a touch too effusively, causing Bill to gaze up only moderately perplexed. Unfazed, Kevin continued, "Playing in the softball game on Sunday?"

Bill pondered the idea briefly then shook his head and said, "Nah, think I'll take the family to the zoo or something."

Ever so nonchalantly Kevin extended his hand toward Bill and handed him Angie's card. "Thought you might want this. For the party I mean."

Bill accepted the card and observed Kevin as he continued his coolly delivered speech.

"Don't think Laura knows her. She's a patient and apparently a fabulous caterer," said Kevin, maintaining his rehearsed level of nonchalance. "She's hot too. Likes older men. If I weren't married...."

"That was the kid who was hanging all over you yesterday?" asked Bill.

In his most sincere voice Kevin said, "Yeah. Actually a bit of a problem for me. Maybe you should take over her case. Doesn't have much weight left to lose."

Bill nodded. "No problem. We don't want any more trouble around here."

Kevin was preparing for a clean getaway, but then Bill said something that provoked an intense response.

"Ever thought of getting another dog?"

Kevin's face cycled through a range of emotions as Bill watched bemused. There was disgust, consternation, jealousy, fear, and apprehension. All he wanted to do was exit Bill's office but he couldn't resist turning to answer his partner before moving back to his own domain. "That damn movable rug was the cause of everything." His voice grew more and more heated. "That incident. With you-know-who. George's fault."

Bill laughed incredulously. How remarkable that Kevin was blaming his infidelity on a dog. "Oh come on," said Bill.

Kevin quickly grew enraged. He strode right up to Bill's desk and though they were inches from each other, his voice grew louder. "He was always in the middle. He understood her. He was a soulmate. And what was I? What was I? I'll tell you what I was. I'll tell you. Yes siree. I was just the chopped liver in the bed on the other side of George. That's what I was. And we all knew it. And he loved it that way."

"Go on—that's nuts," said Bill gazing almost clinically at Kevin. What could possibly be the genuine source of this insane rivalry? He had no clue.

"I come in here to do you a favor," said Kevin, his blue eyes flashing, "And this is how you treat me, deliberately plunging a dagger into my heart and twisting it. Some friend you are."

"Kevin, you're starting to scare me. Can you hear yourself?"

"Oh I hear myself all right. But do you? Do you hear me? If you knew everything you pretended to you wouldn't know half of what you should. Get it?"

"Not even a little bit," said Bill.

Muttering to himself, his comments an inaudible but clearly cranky rumble, Kevin strode back and forth in the office, now and then raising a warning finger toward Bill, who watched him as an adult observes a child mid-tantrum. Eventually Kevin decided to return to work, but as he exited Bill's office, he turned one more time and wagged the warning finger at Bill, who just looked perplexed.

Leaning into the office once more, Kevin said, "You know I'm allergic to dogs."

"No you're not," said Bill.

Kevin's face was stormy and his voice was filled with righteous outrage. He wagged his finger yet another time and said "Well I could be." Then as Bill laughed right in his face—well, at his face—Kevin strode from the room, thinking Bill would get his, delighted to feel completely justified about the plan he had sent into motion. And for years he'd thought of him as a friend—he should have known better.

Chrissy, exhausted after having made an attempt to be Suzy Homemaker and scramble eggs for everyone's breakfast, which admittedly met with some smiles and thank you's, needed to talk to someone, so she'd automatically headed to Zero Tolerance, where there would be someone on a treadmill who wouldn't mind a conversation. They weren't exactly her friends, but more like strangers who'd become casual familiars.

Today she was happy to see the Dominant/submissive couple whom she'd often chatted up before, but whose names escaped her. In her mind they were always labeled as Butch and Wimp. About her age, Butch was a masculine looking woman who carried a riding crop at all times. At this moment the crop sat on the book rest of the treadmill where Butch worked out next to Chrissy. On Butch's other side, Wimp, six years younger, a slender, relatively effeminate looking male, who was working out in a pair of studded leather shorts and a kind of erotic looking pair of studded leather suspenders, which Chrissy knew were not suspenders, but she didn't know what these chest straps were called. They served no purpose as far as she could tell and looked rather comical. As Chrissy talked, Butch and even Wimp listened with rapt attention, although now and then Butch would feel compelled to stop for just a second and whack Wimp on the thigh so he would increase his pace on the treadmill.

Chrissy spoke as though her heart had been completely broken. "I spotted him with his partner's wife. I can't tell you — so humiliating," she sighed.

"Ahh, honey," said Butch with kindly sympathy, whacking Wimp even harder.

Wimp yelped briefly, then swallowed hard as though he were trying to subdue an inappropriate level of arousal there in the gym. "Did you confront him?" Wimp asked.

Chrissy shook her head sadly, "No, but Bill mentioned her, just like it was so cool, so casual, so nothing. But I knew what it was — a dig, aimed right at me."

Whacking Wimp on the back of the thigh, Butch signaled that she wanted him to lift his legs higher as he marched on the treadmill, then said to Chrissy with utter disgust, "Flinging it right in your face like that."

Delighted to be heard and understood, something not even her shrink had provided lately, Chrissy nodded intensely. "Exactly! And I gave up a career for him, to be there with him and his kids, and those kids are vipers half the time."

Wimp continued what appeared to be a quasi-Nazi goosestep on the treadmill but spoke softly in a way that was either paternal or maternal, Chrissy couldn't decide. He said, "Can't really blame the kids, though."

Chrissy considered this for a while, cycling in her mind through all the insults hurled at her by those little monsters and then said, "No, I guess not, of course not. I think he's been putting them up to it though. Can't figure why. Makes no sense."

Butch, whacking Wimp once again and looking with some satisfaction at the streaks of red on his slender thighs, said sternly, "Stop lagging, lazy," then she continued, "Psychological dominance, of course."

Hearing that, Chrissy grew even more concerned, a few tears forming in the corners of her eyes, and then as she continued, she began to sob. "I can't even tell you about the sex. Last night...." Her sobs grew more pronounced as she said, "What was I thinking. I don't know anything any more. And he thinks I don't know what's in that drawer. I know. I know."

Butch and Wimp shared knowing glances. They could picture precisely the sort of deviant torture devices this monster had hidden in a drawer, all without the consent of his partner. That was against the rules. It felt a little erotic to them, but they knew the rules.

"Oh you poor thing," sighed Wimp, who jumped only slightly when Butch cracked the crop against his ass.

Plaintively Chrissy said, "I tell him what I need...yeah...in one ear." For how long had she been begging for Bill's help, for this drug only he could provide, this drug that would be the answer to everything. And what did he do for her? Nothing.

"What a user," said Butch, clearly enraged.

The tears rolled down Chrissy's face. "I've given him the best year of my life."

"He's just begging for it," said Wimp. "Somebody should teach him a lesson."

Butch nodded vigorously, "Yes — then we'd see how quick he puts his foot where his mouth is."

Butch and Wimp drove through the streets of Beverly Hills in their black, Honda CR-V, a popular SUV owned by many people. Both wore black leather and dark glasses. They had been having a serious discussion for several days as they drove around in search of Chrissy's house, but both knew what the outcome would be — whatever Butch decided they should do.

"It must be right around here," said Butch. "I'm sure she said right around here."

"And you're absolutely certain we should be interfering," asked Wimp for about the fiftieth time. "This could turn back around on us. We could get in trouble."

"Look," said Butch, rather exasperatedly, "I know you went to law school for a semester before you opened the flower shop, but we are not going to be persecuted for this. We should be given a medal for this. We're rescuing a woman. We're teaching an abuser a lesson. We're heroes."

"Oh I don't know," said Wimp. "She didn't actually ask us to interfere."

"She did ask. She just didn't realize it." Butch reached out and nudged Wimp and shrieked, "Look—there they are. I knew it was right around here somewhere. That son of a bitch. That Bill is a rotter and he's going to learn a lesson or two. It's time somebody screwed the nipple clamps onto his balls."

As Butch pulled the car over a couple houses down from Bill's, Wimp shook his head. "Nobody mentioned nipple clamps. That would be assault."

"Oh my God," said Butch, "I'm speaking metaphysically, not literately. Now just watch. You'll see I'm correct—it's happening right before our eyes. And ears."

Chrissy had opened the door and Kevin stood beside her. She was in her usual workout gear but gazed out the door carefully before allowing him to exit as though even her attire suggested something clandestine.

"What a waste," sighed Kevin, reaching over to grope Chrissy, who looked left and right as though the neighbors were there forming a circle to point fingers and yell accusatory comments. Nervously, she pushed him away, but he refused to put any space between them.

"He's manhandling her," said Wimp, aghast, as Butch nodded, certain that they were doing the right thing, after observing this abuse in action.

Kevin smiled a lopsided grin at Chrissy, and expecting her to melt into his arms, he leaned in even closer. He casually fondled her ass but to his surprise she jerked away. The woman was quite a challenge, but he was able to handle a challenge.

"Neighbors," she whispered, "For God's sake."

Kevin laughed and reached behind her with his other hand, at an angle that nobody could observe and rubbed her ass, sighing heatedly and then instantly said, "Let's go back inside." Just as he was sliding his hand down her hip along her thigh, she twisted away from him.

Butch was livid. "Oh isn't he just so very menacing. Look at that dopey grin — as though nothing is wrong and everything is just so innocent."

"He gives me the shudders. He's humiliating her in front of the neighbors and she's not even into humiliation." He raised his voice a bit, but as they were a few houses down and the windows were closed, only Butch heard his mock shout, "Consenting adults, asshole!"

Butch put her hand over Wimp's mouth and signaled not to be so loud as she cracked his window a bit so they could hear more clearly. If only she'd parked just a little closer. But she couldn't allow Bill to get a glimpse of them.

Kevin leaned in against Chrissy, pinning her briefly against the doorway. Before she could sidestep him yet again, he reached over and bit her neck. He was certain she was about to moan with pleasure, but no, she pushed him off and said "Ouch!" rather too loudly.

Once more he pressed her against the doorway, rubbing his hand against her breast. This time she pushed harder and he was completely out the door. But he laughed and said in his sexiest voice, "I'll never give up 'til you give in. I can feel it, know you want it."

Wimp and Butch clenched hands tightly. Tears formed in the corner of Wimp's eyes. What an onslaught for them to witness — life was just too cruel. "Did you hear her cry out?" he asked, "He's a brute."

"Don't worry, honey," said Butch, gently patting Wimp's cheek. "We'll take him down a peg. Otherwise she'll never get away from him."

"You're right. He's too devious."

Now that they had a beat on their target, it made sense to Butch to follow him for a while, to learn his routines and his haunts, so off behind Kevin they went as he pulled his Porsche out of Bill's driveway.

Bill felt as though he'd been taken hostage, but what was he to do? He followed along next to Laura as a hyper animated banquet consultant named Betty rhapsodized about the many spectacular events which had taken place there over the years. As she spoke, her arms moved frenetically, her eyes rolled with joy, and numerous happy smiles were interspersed with nervous laughs.

Bill looked about at the dance floor, the many round tables, and considered if this could possibly be a suitable location for a simple birthday party.

"Just picture the magic," sighed Betty, "All your friends in this room — as many as two hundred. For the last party, we hung strings of lights along several of the walls and at the windows. It was so magical. Truly. Magical." She sighed with orgasmic pleasure, then took a deep breath and continued, "We can recommend orchestras, caterers, or do the whole thing for you. Doves even. You could — wait — are you ready for this — you could be the one to pop out of the cake." She patted Laura on the arm.

Laura laughed at that possibility and then realizing there was nobody who would be delighted to see her emerging from any sort of giant cake, sighed deeply and said, "No, the party's for his girlfriend, not my husband."

Nodding rapidly, Betty's eyes glistened with another fantastic idea, "Well then, why be sexist. A handsome guy like you — beefcake jumping out of the cake. Think about it — ohh what magic."

"We have a rickshaw you know," continued Betty before Bill could either think or reply. "And your darling fiancée could ride into her party in that. You could dress as a slave pulling her in, or we could provide slaves." Then she gasped, aware of her potential faux pas, "Not actual slaves of course."

Bill nodded affably, accepting Betty's card, and saying, "We'll think about it and get back to you."

As they walked toward Bill's car, Laura said, "Seemed a bit overblown. Too fiftieth anniversary or salesman of the year."

"I'd say have it at home, but no way to make it a surprise then."

Laura smiled. "A back yard barbecue. Kids running around."

"Lounge chairs. Chickens on a spit," said Bill.

"Couple nice pasta salads," said Laura, "Those are my favorite parties."

Bill nodded, "Me too."

The next place was in Santa Monica, and Bill and Laura enjoyed sitting outdoors on a nice patio, sampling the beautiful food that was set in front of them.

"I know you don't like her, but she really was so sweet. So sunny. Always giving the kids treats when we'd see her at the mall. We had such a good time together — it was like being a family again," sighed Bill.

Laura smiled at him, "Maybe so, but I've just never seen that side of Chrissy. To me she just seems vapid."

"Oh it's this damn diet she's on. Won't listen to a word I say. So wound up I expect to hear her head go pop. She could commit a crime and any jury would let her off."

Laura laughed and nodded, "Diet defense."

"When that woman suggested we jump out of a cake, all I could think would be she'd see the cake and scream like I was torturing her with it. Maybe we're on the wrong track. Maybe we should just have the party at a spa. Serve water ices or something?" Bill grimaced, realizing he wasn't even joking.

Laura's mind had wandered. She spoke almost more to herself than to Bill. "You know, I said no to Kevin about a million times. He was just so determined. And I figured he must care so much, so deeply, to pursue me so intensely. I thought I'd be so safe. Never occurred to me that the thrill was the chase, not me."

Bill saw the sad look cross her face and wondered was Kevin having another affair. If so, he didn't know with whom, though he did suspect one of the nurses at work, more trouble if so. "He's a lot more insecure than you realize. Needs validation," he said kindly.

She sighed and looked down at her hands. "Maybe so. Maybe so."

Kevin was psyched. He strode onto the baseball field like the conquering hero he knew himself to be. He and the Cedars Sinai team were going to teach those UCLA bastards a thing or two. There was nothing like being on a winning team, and Kevin intended to win. He was going to be the star player, today and always.

Kevin was first up to bat and he planned to make it count. He sauntered into place, making sure that the other team knew he was a force. Casually he rubbed his hands in the dirt and wiped them on his pants. He wiggled his butt, not just once but twice. Then he stood there at the plate, sending a searing look toward the other team's pitcher, a dermatologist. In his mind, he practically sneered.

"C'mon there, Barb, we all know you throw like a girl." He laughed at this excellent joke then leaned in toward the catcher and spoke softly, "We had a little thingy. She's still soft on me."

The catcher, clearly a lesbian, shot Kevin a scornful look. Well that was her business.

About twenty feet away, standing behind a large tree with gnarled roots lacing the ground, Butch and Wimp lurked covertly. They might have looked rather out of place in this Beverly Hills park in their omnipresent black leather, but nobody really spotted them — it was a big tree. Wimp held a baseball, and paced in miniscule steps back and forth, still hidden by the tree.

"Get focused," said Butch. "This is your moment. All your energy. And when I say NOW, let it rip."

Wimp clenched his mouth tightly as he wiggled his shoulders, attempting to loosen them up. There was a knot in the pit of his stomach, and he knew it was old memories, high school, gym class, nothing good. He tried to shake them off.

Kevin was enjoying his moment of glory. He wiggled his butt yet again. He clucked his tongue a couple of times. "This is gonna be too easy. I almost feel guilty."

The pitcher was about to wind up, and Kevin noticed a devilish glint in her eye. She must be thinking about that time they shared that quickie. He shot her a crooked smile. Maybe he could tap that again sometime soon. Then, back in the spirit of the game, he said. "Here it comes, a big fat doughnut. Maybe I should just get a cup of coffee to go with it."

Butch was on her game. She was ready for the first confrontation. When a lesson needed to be taught, she was the one to teach it. She muttered to Wimp, "See how he likes being up a tree without a paddle. This is it—get ready….Now!"

Wimp wound up, and with a heave as mighty as he could muster, the ball flew out of his hand, but it was far from the head-denting speedball Butch had envisioned.

At the same moment, the ball left Barb's hand, flying fast and low toward Kevin. It arced in the sky and hurled toward him. As it was coming, Wimp's ball, far short of its target, rolled onto the field toward Kevin, who with self-described lightning reflexes, jumped inward to avoid it hitting his foot. Where had that come from? He looked behind him toward where Butch and Wimp stood invisibly behind a giant tree.

"Quick," said Butch, "Let's get outta here."

Kevin returned his gaze toward the pitch, but it was too late, and the ball smashed into his crotch, causing him to collapse.

"Ball one!" said the umpire.

"Glad she's not soft on me," intoned the catcher.

From where he lay on the ground groaning and scowling, Kevin caught a glimpse of Barb laughing on the pitcher's mound. That bitch!

Butch seethed as she started the car. Turning toward Wimp righteously, she snapped her crop at him. "You totally missed him. You were supposed to hit him."

Wimp, his heart still racing, spoke up with uncharacteristic assertiveness. "Who do you think I am, Ryan Nolan? I'm not um-um-um—Kevin Costner."

Butch remained livid. "Yeah, well—neither is he. And you know what? Neither are you."

Butch pulled the car out and sped away, barely listening to Wimp, who was suggesting that being nutcracked with a softball was punishment enough.

FOUR

"How's Kevin doing today?" asked Bill, wincing a little.

"Still icing the crown jewels. Wouldn't he be okay by now?" asked Laura.

"It can vary. Look it's right down here." They were heading toward Angie's deli, and as they walked past Zero Tolerance, Bill said, "She's a patient."

Spotting a couple smoking, Laura removed a flyer from her bag, handed it to them and said sincerely but with a touch too much emotion, "You're cremating yourselves alive!"

Holding Angie's card, Bill opened the door to It's Delish, and looked around at the small deli, which had only a few customers seated here and there. A counter girl gazed at them with an unremarkable degree of disinterest. After mentioning his reason for being there, she shouted, "Hey, Angie."

It took only a moment for Angie to emerge from the kitchen in her chef's whites. Recognizing Bill, she registered a look of concern. Why was he here? Had something happened to Dr. Flicker? "Oh," she said, "Hello."

Bill smiled at her in a friendly way and said "I didn't realize this was a deli. We could have had lunch here."

"We're planning a party," said Laura.

"Oh, I see," said Angie, relieved. "A party. Somehow I thought you were here because... Well, never mind, come — have a seat."

Bill and Laura sat down and waited only briefly as Angie disappeared and reappeared, bringing a large tray holding many small plates, each containing only a couple nibbles on them. Angie took a seat at the table with them so she could discuss the offerings and make suggestions. With great effort to maintain a polite demeanor, Bill and Laura began tasting the food and their faces revealed only surprise, concealed dislike, and ultimately puzzlement about what they actually were eating.

Angie remained oblivious and said, "Yes, that's right — buffalo pâté."

Laura couldn't quite believe what she was asking, "Isn't this caramel inside this meatball?"

Angie smiled excitedly. "Yes! Do you like it? I haven't tasted most of these items — the diet you know — but I'm going for real cutting edge cuisine. Oblivious to what was transpiring behind her, Angie didn't notice as Butch and Wimp at a neighboring table gazed at each other with disgust. Butch began coughing and almost turned green. Suspiciously, Wimp lifted his plate and sniffed it before almost gagging. Together they rose, as she tossed a bill onto the table and they hightailed it out of the deli.

"You know," mused Bill softly, "Something a bit more simple might be best. Chinese chicken salad."

"Poached salmon," added Laura.

Enthused, Angie replied, "I just created a saffron-curry sauce with chopped octopus and deep fried cilantro."

"Maybe on the side," said Laura politely.

Chrissy was having a horrifically frustrating conversation with someone she was certain was a brain dead liar. "Yes, I *do* want to talk to the manager," she said with extreme irritation, "It's just impossible for me to take you seriously. There's no way you didn't notice. You're not disabled, are you?"

Nonplussed, the little idiot said, "I'll get Joan."

"Hurry, will you," said Chrissy, seething. She untied a jaunty bandana knotted around her neck and mopped her brow with it. Almost gasping for air, she wondered would she faint. Clutching one of the exercise machines, she lowered herself down onto it, then in an act of extreme desperation pressed the bandana over her face, covering mouth and nose. She took several breaths, growing even more agitated. It didn't help. It didn't help. Air, she thought, oh clean air.

Joan arrived and leaned over her with an aura of deep concern. She smiled and patted Chrissy on the shoulder. "Are you all right?" she asked.

With what appeared to be SARS level terror, Chrissy removed the bandana from her face and attempted to breathe but immediately began choking and gasping. In between gasps for unpolluted air, she managed to squeeze out a few words, "This place reeks!"

Joan's demeanor instantly became calm. She said placatingly, "We clean the locker rooms with Clorox. Also the towels. People are sweating, though, but of course it is a gym." As Joan spoke, a couple of guys dripping sweat passed and she glanced toward them trying to make her point without alerting them.

Growing more and more deeply panic-stricken, Chrissy began waving her arms around wildly as though she were attempting to communicate via sign language to someone in a foreign country. She tried to take a deep breath to regain her inner balance, but every time she did the smell was like a massive assault to her brain. Finally she gasped and jerkily ejected the words as though they were Pez shooting out of a dispenser.

"No, no, no. Sweat is normal. Sweat is good. Wholesome, even." She held the bandana over her mouth for a few seconds and raised her index finger to Joan, indicating she would resume speaking as soon as she could manage it. Finally she said, "I'm talking about the *smell.*" She glared at Joan. "Do not tell me you don't smell it." Chrissy waived her arm in the direction of the door and beyond.

Joan looked toward the door rather perplexed and then as a show of good faith, took a deep breath. Then she returned her gaze to Chrissy, who immediately began speaking in a rush of words.

"I mean the *food.* I'm smelling ratatouille with some sort of chocolate. Lamb—and a great deal of cinnamon." She gagged visibly as she continued, "Deep frying...."

A look of recognition crossed Joan's face at last. "Oh," she said softly, "You mean the deli down the way." She observed Chrissy nodding vigorously, the bandana covering her nose and mouth, but her eyes, which were pretty much all she'd left uncovered, conveyed deep horror. Joan continued even more calmly, "That's not something we can control." Patting Chrissy on the shoulder, she said, "You certainly have an acute sense of smell."

Chrissy shrugged Joan's hand off her arm, then said with rage, "How are people supposed to concentrate on what's important with that smell? They write horror movies about smells like those. Didn't you ever read Edgar Allen Pope? He wrote horror stories about religion." Chrissy paused, thinking wait, wait, wasn't there a bird involved, some kind of black chicken, but she couldn't be sure of anything and the point was to make her point, so with confidence she added, "And bad smells."

Joan glanced up at the ceiling, trying to place that name, but she couldn't. Then she said, "We can't control the neighbors. Surely you understand that."

Chrissy flailed about, alternately waving her hands and pressing the bandana to her face. "I can't breathe in here. Oh my God! What if I have to quit this gym?"

Joan heard the word quit and her face registered worry only for a moment. The members had contracts. Nobody could quit. But still, this woman could make some trouble. People were certainly gazing at them right now.

Chrissy continued, "This place is my oasis. I could have a breakdown."

"I can't tell you how sorry I am about all this," said Joan, echoing what she'd heard an army of customer service reps say every time she made a call to complain about anything. "I apologize. Please accept my apologies."

"Apologies?" asked Chrissy with utter disgust.

"I'm going to look into this," said Joan. "And whatever I can do to solve this problem I will. Zero Tolerance, right?"

"Yes!" said Chrissy, semi-placated. "Zero Tolerance."

Feeling marginally better but unwilling to leave this travesty in the hands of someone else, Chrissy dressed and marched down the street in the direction from which all the toxicity emanated. She would take whatever steps were necessary. Envisioning a protest march of similarly disgusted gym patrons holding signs, she knew it wouldn't be long before that deli closed its doors and something innocuous took its place. Maybe a nice greeting card shop.

She looked at the deli, a hole in the wall really, well a charming hole in the wall, called It's Delish. Delish indeed. More like de-frightful. Just as Chrissy was about to stride into the deli with an air of righteous authority, seething, and muttering some of the precise words she'd use when the confrontation took place, she noticed to her horror that there inside sat Bill with Laura and she was about to pop a bite of food into his mouth. His expression told the tale—he looked enraptured, anticipatory—and oddly a little terrified. What did that mean? What sort of hold over him did that cold, controlling bitch have?

Chrissy stopped dead. Now what? Quickly she turned to walk away, but something pulled her back. So there she was outside that toxic pit, marching back and forth like a hypnotized soldier.

Before she could formulate a strategy, Bill and Laura rose. They were moving! They would see her! Quickly Chrissy turned and walked several paces away from the deli and dashed into another shop. Oh no! It was Godiva.

The girls inside smiled and greeted her with warmth and friendliness. "Care for a sample?" one asked sweetly. As if. As if. The utter gall.

"Yeah you'd like that, wouldn't you? You enslavers of women. You devils in aprons. You monsters. This place is a menace. It should be closed down. They all should be closed down. And you can bet I know what I'm talking about." Chrissy burst into tears as she gazed at a tray of samples being offered to her. "Don't shove that in my face!" she commanded. As she wept, she crumpled onto the floor, deep in tears while the salesgirls looked to each other, clueless about what to do. "I just can't get away from you," Chrissy sobbed, and then she finally said the word, the word she'd vowed never to say again, "And all that deliciousness."

Just as one of the girls was reaching out to offer her a kindly pat on the back and the other was again about to extend the sample tray toward her, Chrissy rose, violently held out both hands in the sign of the cross, just as someone holding a vampire at bay might, and she ran from the store.

She gazed down the street, where she could clearly see Bill and Laura strolling as though they hadn't a care in the world. Life sucked, she thought. Then she turned and walked toward her car.

Bill and Laura glanced at each other, both a bit queasy. "They don't usually put curry in cake frosting, do they?" he asked.

Looking nauseated, Laura said, "Chocolate in eggplant? The only wine you could serve with that food would be Alka Seltzer."

Ben was feeling good about himself. Taking Clint up on his offer to be his trainer was a good idea. He was already looking more buff, and he felt better too, more alive. Who knew that joining a gym could be so entertaining? He and Clint were marching up and down on Stairmasters and talking causally while observing a girl with an oddly familiar voice having what appeared to be a psychotic break.

"Woah, dude," said Clint, "Ketosis, not good, not good."

"I think she's on something, hopped up. Cocaine, maybe?"

"Herbal diet pills," said Clint, "Super toxic. Hope she snaps out of it. C'mon, let's hit the weights."

Ben followed Clint into the weight room and mimicked everything he did, only with smaller weights. "You know, I think this is working," he said happily, seeing an actual bicep in the mirror.

"Of course it's working," said Clint. "That's why they call it working out. Cause it works."

"I just hope Angie starts noticing," sighed Ben. "I'm taking her to the movies tonight."

"Well it's a date, so that can't be bad, can it," said Clint, supportively.

"Only if she thinks it's a date, but I have a feeling she doesn't."

"Dude, I know you're hot for this girl, but I just don't get it. There's something I learned on PBS and I never forgot it."

Ben was surprised. He'd never seen Clint watching anything but porn or the Olympics. "PBS?" he asked.

"Did you know there are more women on the planet than dudes? It's a known fact. And do you know why this is?"

Ben nodded, "Because the XX chromosome is statistically favored over the XY."

Clint shook off that bit of useless psychobabble and said, "It's cause dudes need options. If a babe says no, there are always more who say yes. Otherwise there would be an epidemic." Clint scowled at Ben's look of disbelief. "Yes," he continued, "An epidemic—of blue balls. Nature doesn't want that because dudes do all the building and nobody can drive a crane with blue balls."

Ben tried to conceal his laughter but he couldn't and Clint didn't even glare at him. They'd been friends for too long. "All I'm saying is go for what you want but don't let it ruin your life. For all you know there's another girl way hotter than Angie who'd be lots less trouble. I'll fix you up if you want. At least you'd have something to compare her with. Or we can go out together. Just think about it."

Ben nodded. "You're a great friend, Clint. Thanks for the offer. But first shouldn't I try the advice you gave me the other day? Show her I'm straight, be a little macho—I mean I've been in love with this girl since the third grade."

Clint shrugged. "Ok, bud, maybe it'll finally click. You must be gangbusters in bed with stamina like that."

Ben smiled, happy to think of himself as gangbusters in bed. Maybe he could be. Right now, though, he was just relieved that nobody was asking him to drive a crane.

Angie stood happily in line at the revival theater, next to Ben, who carried a shopping bag from a book store. He was the one person to whom she could confide everything. Her eyes glowed brightly as she recounted her most recent experience with Dr. Flicker. "And he was practically all over me. I'm fearless around him. I say things I'd never have the nerve to say to anyone else. It feels so deep, so intense."

This wasn't going at all the way it should. Angie hadn't even noticed his new clothes or the fact that his sleeves were rolled up to display his newly empowered biceps. Ben had to do something, so when a decently sexy woman passed them he took a chance. "Woah!" he said in his best Clint imitation. "Look at her! She's hot! You think she'd go for me?" Then he carefully scrutinized Angie to see if she presented the hoped for reaction. Was that the tiniest glint of insecurity? Did she seem a little jealous?

"Sure she would," said Angie. "Go talk to her."

Oh no! Ben's heart lurched. "What about you," he said, trying to lead the conversation back to where it belonged.

But uncomprehending of his true meaning, Angie said, "Oh don't worry about me—I can take a cab home. You deserve to meet a nice woman."

Ben sighed. "No, no.... I meant.... Geeez.... I mean.... Like, um. Well. Never mind, um, I mean, here, open this present."

To Angie's surprise, Ben pulled a nicely wrapped present from his shopping bag and handed it to her. She carefully removed the paper then read the title out loud.

"*Off Daddy's Lap – Conquering the Electra Complex*. Hmm. This looks….interesting. Lotta great recipes in here I bet." Then as he looked bewildered, she laughed, and said, "You're such a sweetie."

Angie reached over to hug Ben, and he glowed and hugged her back even more tightly. She gently kissed his cheek and he could feel the color rising in his face.

She jumped away from him and said, "Look, we're going in. I've never seen *Lolita*. What's it about?"

Bill was enjoying an evening with the family in front of the television. Chrissy seemed calm enough and he liked having her nestled in the crook of his arm. He was thinking vaguely about the party he was planning and hoping that everything was once again back on track.

Will had found a creative use for the Barbie Dream Car and repeatedly he smashed it into the Barbie Dream House as Candy attempted with little success to wrench it away from him. Bill glanced at them now and then.

Chrissy was attempting to talk about her future, about the possibility of her having a career. "What if it isn't enough?" she asked Bill sincerely, "Don't you think I should have something to fall back on? I'm not ever going back to…."

Bill smiled at her and said, "I know the kids love having you here when they come home from school."

Candy and Will stopped their wrestling briefly to glance at each other and to roll their eyes.

"But sweetheart," continued Bill, "Sure, get a job if you want one."

Chrissy didn't know whether to consider this a supportive gesture or one designed to avoid palimony when Bill's affair with his partner's wife came to light and everything crashed and burned. "I just don't know what I'd do," she mused.

Bill spoke up and said "Maybe you'd feel more fulfilled if you'd stop...."

Before he could continue, Chrissy interrupted, "How about a Koush Koush distributorship?"

"I told you," said Bill far less charitably, "That drug is never coming to the U.S."

Unwilling to hear his excuses yet again but also determined not to set him off, Chrissy said congenially, "What about an herbal version?"

By this time Will had taken one of Candy's Barbies and had wrapped its hair around a rear wheel of the Barbie Dream Car and was dragging the doll behind the car. Candy began wailing in increasing volume.

"Stop it!" said Bill to Chrissy. "Enough with the Koush Koush! It's all you ever talk about. No more, *please*. Enough!"

"Daddy," screamed Candy.

"Will," said Bill sternly.

Candy shoved Will with her shoulder and managed to wrench the Barbie out from the wheel of the car, but half of her hair was left wedged into the wheel. Will began laughing at the half-bald Barbie as Candy screamed and wept.

Chrissy leapt to her feet, clearly displeased. "That's enough!" she said with authority. Pointing toward Will, she said, "You! On the Stairmaster. Now." Will glanced at his dad, who shrugged, so he decided uncharacteristically to obey. Then Chrissy pointed at Candy and said, "You! On the rowing machine."

"Hey!" protested Candy, "I'm not the criminal here. Look at my Barbie." She thrust the half-bald doll toward her father.

Chrissy smiled as though the light had finally dawned. "That's it!" she said excitedly. "I'll work at the gym—or one of those diet centers. Can you imagine a better plan?"

Bill rose, kissed her on the cheek and nodded, smiling. "Anyone want ice cream?" he asked pleasantly.

Chrissy, aghast, intoned, "Bill!" But he was already on the way to the kitchen.

FIVE

Angie was engaged in a staring match with Nurse Leona, who really seemed to be against her. She provided such a sober atmosphere in the examining room that it created a wall between herself and Kevin, a wall Angie was certain was destined to topple any day now. She thought if she stared hard and long enough, Leona would exit the room, leaving her alone when Kevin arrived. Her focus was so intense that she almost didn't notice when Dr. Masters instead of Dr. Flicker entered the room.

Bill smiled pleasantly at Angie and said, "Hello, Ms. Antimangia. Nice to see you again."

Angie didn't bother to hide the shock that registered on her face, nor the disappointment. "Where's Kev — Dr. Flicker?" she asked with irritation.

"He's been so swamped lately, I've taken over some of his cases. I hope you don't mind," said Bill, again very pleasantly. Angie was unable to think of a reply as he continued, "I see you're doing great, as usual."

She sat there, frustrated and sad as he went through the motions of listening to her heart, checking her pulse, and when all the vitals were ascertained, he patted her kindly on the shoulder. "Looking great, just great."

Angie sighed, "I was sorry you didn't like my food."

Bill smiled. "I was going to call you — let's talk in my office."

As Angie took a seat opposite Bill, he worked to neutralize her hurt feelings. His face, unfailingly kind, conveyed a sense of paternal goodness. "I'm not much of a sophisticated eater. I just like plain, simple food, so really I'm not the best judge of your amazing cuisine."

Angie brightened, "Oh. I see."

Bill smiled at her and was happy to see her face grow less stormy. "But if you'd be willing to do some simple, sort of traditional things, no reason at all why we wouldn't love to have you cater it. Of course it's probably not fair to ask you to do that—no challenge to the artist in you. So I'll understand if...."

Angie smiled in return. He was nice. And very handsome. "No, no," she said, "Sure, I'd love to do it. Doesn't have to be cutting edge to be fabulous."

"Well, great." Bill paused to look down at her chart, then asked, "So—how's the diet going? Having any issues with your new, thinner body?"

"I don't really feel all that different. I thought I would. I'm still surprised when people look—and don't throw up." Angie laughed but they both knew she wasn't really making a joke.

"Being thinner can't rid you of problems. All it can change is your dress size."

Angie stopped for a moment to think about this, but it wasn't anything she didn't already know. "I catch a glimpse of myself in mirrors or store windows and I think, who's that—and then I remember—it's me. Amazing." She grew quiet briefly while he waited and she was surprised to note that he was actually listening, actually participating in the conversation. "At least I got a handle on the food thing. I never taste anything I cook. Used to taste or snack all day long."

"Interesting," said Bill. "So. Let's talk about anger."

"Anger?" asked Angie.

"Are you still angry at your dad?"

"Oh," said Angie, surprised, "You knew." Had he read that in her file? Did Kevin tell him that? "Other day I brought him some homemade Gelato and he didn't even take it."

"Have you talked to him about this?" asked Bill gently.

Angie drew in her breath sharply. "Oh I couldn't do that. Nobody talks to Daddy. I'd have to get arrested to get his attention."

"Yes you can," said Bill encouragingly. "I have two suggestions. First, talk to your dad. Secondly, go back to the deli and taste very small bites of what you're cooking. And then at mealtime adjust your food a bit to compensate and of course maintain correct levels of exercise. I think you'll discover something interesting."

"What?"

Bill smiled. "We'll discuss it next time."

Angie was highly agitated as she left the office. Dr. Masters was a nice man but he clearly was crazy and that wasn't even the whole problem. The problem was her plan was being foiled. And she did not intend to give up—she was no quitter. So she left the building and waited out front, pacing now and then and intermittently checking her watch—he would surely be going out to lunch shortly. And there he was!

Kevin walked out of the office building and toward his Porsche, but Angie stepped right up to him with a gleaming but insecure smile.

"Kevin! Dr. Flicker," she called.

He strained to recall her name, but couldn't, then smoothly said, "Well, hi. What are you doing here?"

Angie sounded so sorrowful as she asked, "Are you mad at me?"

"Of course not," Kevin replied. He noticed a familiar looking black Honda cruising by, and briefly he turned in the direction of the vehicle, but it sped away. Did he know that car?

Angie took his absorption as a sign. "You're not telling me something. I can feel it."

Kevin knew an out when he was presented with one. Conspiratorially he said, "I have to be extra careful now. People are watching me." He glanced in the direction in which the Honda had gone. "Holding things over my head. Plotting. They know about...."

Wide eyed, Angie asked, "About us?"

"You can't imagine how serious Dr. Masters is. He sees us together and he worries." Kevin smiled at her in his most beguiling way and continued, "Too hard to hide chemistry like ours."

Angie quivered a little, something which Kevin did not fail to notice.

His eyes narrowed and he said, "Problem is nobody has ever tempted him. I just wish. Well, I shouldn't say it. I'll just stop here."

The air rushed from Angie's throat as she sighed, "Oh no, don't stop. Tell me everything."

Kevin looked to the right and the left as though he were making sure he was not being overheard or spotted. "Ok. I wish someone would come along and seduce his ass." He gulped a few times, then said, "Oh, please excuse me."

"No, no, I'm here for you, Kevin. Do you still have my number?" Kevin looked so worried, Angie didn't want to trouble him, so she pulled another card from her purse and scribbled her home number on the back before giving it to him. "Here—take this one."

Kevin shook his head sadly. "I'm just not free to come and go. If only Bill could have a taste of what I feel with you."

Thrilled, Angie sighed and glowed with the flattery, then came back to earth, saying, "I think he's a quack. He's nothing compared to you. He told me to eat—to taste again."

"Really?" asked Kevin, seemingly shocked, then he did an about face and calmly said, "Maybe you should try his approach. Get on his good side." He scrutinized Angie's face, but nothing seemed amiss, so he continued, "Oh no, I could never ask you to…."

Kevin felt good about the way that encounter had gone. If he had planned it precisely it couldn't have gone any better than it had naturally. Soon things would be happening, thanks to his cleverness and skills with women. It was exciting to wait and watch as the whole thing whirled into being. And wouldn't Bill be amusing when caught with his pants down for a change.

He drove his Porsche leisurely, while he talked on his cell phone. "It's all in motion now, baby. It's an unstoppable force, like fudge boiling over." Wanting to enjoy the thrills and chills of the conversation, he pulled into an empty space and just sat there, talking.

Conveniently parked several cars behind Kevin were Butch and Wimp. Butch rapped her fingers rhythmically on the steering wheel as Wimp repeatedly turned to look at a parcel in the back seat.

"I asked you to hold that steady between your legs on the floor up here," said Butch with no small degree of irritation.

Wimp shook his head with fear and apprehension. "I didn't fight in any wars cause I didn't want my balls blown off. Do you think I would let that happen here in Beverly Hills?"

Butch reached for her crop. He had been getting increasingly bold and cheeky and she knew she should put a stop to it immediately. Their whole relationship was going downhill because of this quest, but she knew she couldn't simply abandon that poor gym girl who was so at the mercy of this snake.

"We're gonna make a point today," she said. "If he can't stand the heat, he should stay out of the bedroom!"

Kevin had relaxed back against the leather seat of his Porsche and was enjoying the way the conversation was going. "Until you moan. Until you whimper and beg me to stop, no to never stop." He listened as Chrissy's voice got that thready, raspy quality that so turned him on, then he continued, "I'm going to take some of those licorice whips…." He paused again then responded to her query, "Red." And then another pause, followed by "Okay, red *and* black."

Wimp had detached his seatbelt and gingerly set the tote bag between him and Butch as they each turned their full attention toward it and the last minute tinkering Butch had to do. Dangling a few tools from the very edge of his fingers as though he were holding something nauseatingly drippy or gooey, he set them down on his lap. Butch faced the middle of the car and focused completely on what she was doing. She knew it would be no problem after all her years working in studio FX and prop departments. If she could build fireworks—and she could—she could certainly do this.

Wimp's hands clearly trembled. "Are you really so sure we should go this far," he asked. "We could get into tr...."

Clenching the needle nosed pliers, Butch looked up and glared at him for what felt like the zillionth time. "We're taking a stand."

Wimp shook his head. "I just don't want to cross the line."

Butch grew even more livid. "That man is an enslaver of women. He's the one who's crossed the line and now he's gonna hang from it."

Kevin was cooing into the phone, "Yes," he sighed in his sexiest voice, "Gummy bears." He couldn't take it any longer. "I'm coming over there."

Kevin abruptly pulled out into traffic and sped away as an identical Porsche smoothly pulled into his vacated space. The doors opened and a couple exited the car. She was elegant but no beauty and she spoke with an irritating Valley girl accent. She carried an Ipad, onto which she intermittently typed and flipped through information. Her companion was dressed and sounded like a New York wise guy, with that sleek, sharp, shiny suit and a certain prancing air. His accent was so thick it was almost impossible to understand him.

As they walked toward a restaurant, she said flirtatiously, "Um, like, I totally knew you were totally right for us the moment I saw you—I mean totally." He gazed at her like Mr. Very Cool, and swaggered even more, patting what appeared to be a bulge in his jacket pocket, then snapping his sunglasses.

"Of cauze you did," he said, "I din't wawk in yaw daw fwaw nuttin'. I knoo what daw it wuz and whut you waunted and I wuz the guy tah do it. No questyuns axed."

She shivered a little with expectation and they both entered the bistro and disappeared from sight.

Wimp and Butch were deep in concentration but shortly Butch nodded, indicating everything was ready. She gestured toward the car and nodded at Wimp. "Ok, do just what I told you."

Wimp grimaced and then exited the Honda, casually but neurotically walking toward the Porsche. Stopping constantly to gaze around for potential hazards, he followed Butch's directive and planted some sticky stuff at the bumper and under fenders, always jumping back from the car each time. He glanced at his watch in dread, then hightailed it back to their vehicle.

"Quick," he said terrified, "Get outta here. Go. Go. Go."

Butch sneered and said, "Wait."

Then it came, a loud pop, and the midsized explosion Butch had so carefully engineered. She laughed with glee, then held her hand up for Wimp to slap, and he attempted to fist bump her and then she flicked both hands in exasperation at him. He wasn't that young, but he never got the high five. Why did she bother.

Preparing to drive away, Butch noticed the wise guy and his companion running hysterically out of the bistro toward the car.

Butch, horrified, looked toward Wimp, who was even more upset than the owners of the Porsche. "What? What? What?" Then she pulled the car out of their spot and sped away.

Standing by the flaming Porsche, the woman was stunned to observe her companion, who in the space of seconds had transformed from a macho New York wise guy into a hysterical Valley boy. His gestures had gone instantly from macho and assured to effeminate and panic-stricken.

He waved and flailed toward two cops and some firemen who'd arrived on the scene almost instantly. "Oh officers! Officers! Over here! I'm dying, I'm dying. Bobby's car, I wasn't even supposed to drive it, now look at it. Doesn't it break your heart? I may need medical attention. I could very well be in shock. And what will I tell Bobby? I'll be sleeping on the couch for a year."

The woman looked toward him, embarrassed that she'd made such a fuss over him, chagrinned that she'd envisioned more happening between them during the shooting. "What happened to your New York ..."

Suddenly realizing that he'd fallen totally out of character, the wise guy pulled himself together and attempted to regain the macho that had dissolved in the explosion. "I still get the part, right?"

SIX

Laura parked in front of a festively decorated house, several clusters of balloons out front indicating that something big was happening here today. It was—her daughter Julie's good friend Jessica was turning nine and just as Laura was about to enter the house to pick Julie up, she and Candy stepped outside. Both girls giggled and smiled happily, their faces painted to resemble cats. They each held balloons, goodie bags and were excitedly talking.

"Daddy!" yelled Candy, and Laura turned and spotted Bill, exiting his car and walking toward the girls. Candy raced toward Bill and hugged him tightly. He waved toward Laura, smiling.

"Hiya cat women!" he said cheerfully, "Did you have fun?"

Candy nodded vigorously. "Yes, it was much better than Cheryl's party. Nobody threw up!"

Bill laughed. "That's a relief."

Laura smiled at the girls and their happy faces, then turned to Bill and asked, "Have some time? I have an idea."

Laura left her car parked on the street and the four of them took off in Bill's car toward Santa Monica. As they turned onto the pier and walked toward the carousel, both girls squealed, "Merry-go-round."

The antique carousel with its beautifully restored horses and benches on the celebrated Santa Monica pier was a local treasure. Only more recently had the city added an amusement park on the pier, making it an even more popular spot.

The girls raced toward the ticket booth as Laura spoke softly to Bill, "What do you think?" Then she silently mouthed the word, "Party?"

Bill nodded and smiled, answering, "It's perfect. I love it!"

"I love it too," squealed Candy. "Let's ride a bunch of times!"

Bill paid for eight tickets and they all climbed up onto horses, peacefully going up and down as the nostalgic carousel music played. The girls were delighted when the ride ended and Bill held up another set of tickets so they could do it all over again.

When the girls suggested a ride on the roller coaster, Bill and Laura looked at each other cautiously. Bill shook his head, "Little girls who've been eating cupcakes and candy all day probably don't belong on a roller coaster. We don't want to break that throw up record today, do we?"

Candy shrugged. She didn't like throwing up but she didn't want the day to end.

"What if we go stroll along the Promenade for a while," suggested Laura.

"Strolling," said Julie.

"Strolling is good," said Candy.

Third Street had long been designated a walking area, no cars allowed, and in the last two decades had become the prime gathering spot of the district. Couples went on dates, parents took children to see the amateur performers who themselves were there in hopes of being seen by someone in the entertainment industry. Moviegoers lined up and ate excellent pizza, and shoppers walked the several blocks, accumulating purchases as they went. There were restaurants to suit every palate and pocket book and it was in general a fun place to stroll.

"We're outside and no smoking," enthused Laura. "Not allowed here. Fantastic."

Candy and Julie demanded to stop and offer coins to a monkey with his organ grinder—they laughed as the monkey took the money right from their hands and begged for more coins so he wouldn't walk away.

They continued their stroll and Laura stopped to listen to a little girl singing—she couldn't have been more than twelve. She had a boom box with her, and apparently her dad was her manager. He'd cue up the music and she'd sing, a microphone comfortably in her hand. The girls were less entranced and pulled on their parents to move forward.

"Ohh," enthused Julie, "Tattoos."

Bill scowled, but Candy squealed too. "Just how much paint do you need on your skin in one day?" Bill asked.

Laura laughed. "Never enough," she said. "These wash right off, don't they?" Laura asked the hopeful artist, who was busy showing the girls all the designs. When she nodded, Laura looked to Bill, who also nodded and soon enough the girls were debating where to put this newest ink.

Julie held up her ankle, "I think flowers right here, like an ankle bracelet. One I won't lose!"

"Cool idea," said Candy. "I'm gonna have this heart, right here on my arm." Bill winced a little as he saw

Candy had chosen a blue heart with the word *Mom* in pink in the middle.

Laura touched Bill gently on the arm and both parents stood silently, watching their little girls being decorated as the girls oohed and aahed with excitement. Just as the artist was finishing, Laura observed a hippie girl passing, holding a young puppy.

"Oh look," said Laura, "Doesn't he just remind you of...." Laura gazed tenderly at the puppy as the girl stopped and allowed everyone to pat him. Then she pointed a few steps down, toward where the SPCA had set up a table for pet adoptions.

"Be very gentle," said Laura to the girls, who were busy patting the puppies who were corralled in a fenced area on top of a long table.

"Pat him, Mommy," said Julie. "It's okay. He doesn't mind."

Laura reached down and picked up one of the puppies, snuggling it tightly under her chin and sighing sweetly. "Ohh you're such a little doll, such a little love bug," Laura cooed.

Bill thought of Kevin, and said cautiously, "Are you sure?"

Laura tried to return the puppy to the coral but she just couldn't. She looked helplessly at Bill, who had already made a donation and bought a leash. Julie and Candy pranced along beside Laura, taking turns petting the puppy.

"Should we call him George II?" asked Laura.

Bill took the dog from her arms briefly and lifted it, scrutinizing its privates. He laughed, "Georgette," he said.

"No!" said Laura laughing back at him, "Gracie!"

They stopped again at a sunglass cart where the girls were busy trying on the most outrageous designs, not at all designed for children. Julie reached out and set some heart shaped, diamond trimmed glasses onto Gracie's nose and the dog shook her head but seemed to be smiling. "She needs these," insisted Julie.

"No, she doesn't," said Bill and Laura simultaneously.

Chrissy hadn't felt this good in a long, long time. Her life was actually moving forward. This morning when she dressed in her favorite tailored suit, she was excited to notice how great she looked — and that the suit seemed substantially looser than it had the last time she'd worn it. This was her big day. She'd walked into the diet center like she owned the place and had been hired on the spot. Now she would have something of her own, something great, and she'd be able to help and inspire other people.

She glanced around the room. Everything was in place for her first session. She'd refilled the pamphlets station. The doctor's scale had been dusted — by someone else of course, not by a superstar like herself. She was here to motivate people, not to dust. It was a huge step up. The bulletin board was nicely organized, thanks to her, and it contained all the weight loss information the center offered. She'd even added some material on her own, downloaded and printed at home. A second bulletin board boasted a collection of before and after photos. Those were the success stories. Chrissy could just imagine how many success stories she would create and all the grateful people who would walk into their healthier, thinner lives, thanks to her wisdom, knowledge, and most of all experience. Nobody knew more about this subject than she did. Well, of course Bill knew a lot. But he only knew it from the outside. She was right here in the trenches. And she'd lived it. Lived it all her life.

Seated in chairs in the big sharing circle, wearing name tags, first name only of course, were half a dozen fatties. No, Chrissy wouldn't even think of them like that—they were future thin people. All she had to do was show them the way and the light. She was ready. These were people who were like her, who wanted what she wanted. They were going to be her best friends some day, she knew it—and she would be their mentor.

Chrissy slipped closer into the room, taking a moment to listen to what was being said in the sharing circle. She just knew it was something right on, something inspirational. But wait....

A woman tagged Glenda was whining almost, speaking with resignation, "I couldn't help it. The kids gave me the candy. It was love, not just food."

Then someone labeled Jean chimed in and said sympathetically, "It's so hard sometimes because you take care of them, but who takes care of you."

A gruff looking middle-aged guy called Lou spoke up with a crusty voice, "These pre-packaged dinners are so small. I like a nice steak...."

Chrissy was aghast. They were heathens! They needed her desperately and where was she? She was right here, ready, willing and able to charge into the group and get these people in order. "What am I hearing?" she said sternly. She stomped into the circle and walked around, stopping briefly in front of each dieter, glaring, then moving on. "You people are *losers!* Except where your diets are concerned."

She took a full minute for this to penetrate, then she marched toward Glenda and stood staring at her, making and holding that all-important eye contact. "Is candy important?" she sneered angrily, and snidely continued, "From the *kids?*" She wagged a finger at Glenda and said sternly, "No! It isn't!"

She walked around the circle once again. Then she zeroed in on Lou. Her eyes narrowed. Her lips clenched. "Next you're going to be whining you miss your beer."

She raised a fist and shook it with passion. Then, looking them all in the eyes, she said, "Am I gonna hear next that you don't want to get rid of your size fifty jeans?" Glaring intensely, she continued, "What's wrong with you people?"

Just at that moment, Chrissy's supervisor, a girl of only twenty-five, pretty, youthful, and naturally slender, gazed in the room. This was exciting. Chrissy had gotten off to a fabulous start and now Elise could see her in action. She smelled a promotion coming. And many newly thin people following her to the ends of the earth. She knew what to do: amp it up a little.

With evangelical fervor, Chrissy continued, pacing, stopping, glaring, and gazing into eyes that began to mist over, eyes that held an occasional tear, or a newly felt rage. "Do you want to look like beached whales for the rest of your lives?" Chrissy snapped her fingers toward the fattest person in the circle and continued, "You think you'll get love that way? You think you'll get *sex* that way?" She made a gesture of questionable taste then continued, marching with increased vigor and glaring even more deeply at her clients. "Your husbands — and wives — are probably too scared to have sex with you. Afraid you'll roll over on them. SPLAT!" She clapped her hands together for emphasis.

Glenda and Jean rose at that moment and attempted to flee.

Her supervisor coughed, then spoke up, "Excuse me, Chrissy, could I see you for a minute? Take a short break everyone, won't you. We have some great pamphlets right over there." Gently, Elise led Glenda and Jean back to their seats.

Chrissy, excited about her imminent promotion, followed Elise toward the back, where the offices were. In the background she could hear the conversation. Jean, grown foolishly bold without Chrissy there to keep her in line, said, "This is worse than EST."

Lou, sounding less gruff and more tremulous, said, "The army was kinder."

But so what. Chrissy would whip them into shape in no time. This was like a calling — she had been led here and now she would rock it.

The people in the sharing circle sat and watched the drama through the window into the back office. Chrissy seemed to be shaking her fist at Elise.

"I hope she doesn't kill her," said Glenda. "We'll never get out alive otherwise."

Chrissy was enraged. That moron Elise who was supposed to fawn all over her and offer a promotion was instead firing her. This place was for losers. "Yeah," said Chrissy, "Well I hope you gain fifty pounds and your implants burst!"

She stormed out the door as Elise looked down quizzically at her b-cup.

Livid, Chrissy slammed an exercise duffel bag into the trunk then kicked the car a few times but it made her feel no better. How was she going to do anything if the world was filled with morons? Didn't it seem lately that she met more and more morons? They were taking over the planet. She entered the car and slammed the door, speeding away, seething and thinking about morons.

Bill did what he often did after work. When most other men were out for drinks with colleagues, dashing off for a quickie with a mistress, or even hastening home to a beloved wife, Bill meandered through the supermarket. He could cook—after a fashion—well he could almost cook, that's what he'd say if anyone asked. He could read a package and he could probably follow a recipe, but he didn't try that often. He could cook hamburger and add sauce and make spaghetti. He could add stuff to packaged salads. He could grill, of course, because grilling was a man's birthright, a result of having evolved from cave dwellers. It wasn't about cooking, however, it was about the meander, the stroll through the market, the aisles with all the boxes, the sense that here lay life and sustenance. In the mornings he visited JoEllen and longed for the life they shared. In the evenings he visited the market.

He'd felt better about himself and about life in general since he began making breakfasts and dinners for the kids. Yes, he had to deal with Chrissy's intolerance of anything not in the category of lettuce, but all he had to do was speak sternly and she would back off. That was odd, wasn't it? Did she seem different? He wondered, but he seldom stopped long enough to ponder the question seriously. He suspected there was much about Chrissy and her current odd behavior that he could unravel with a little prodding but it was his desire lately not to explore, not to question, just to drift. It seemed so much less taxing.

Tonight he would grill some steaks. Recently he discovered that you could grill vegetables such as peppers and even—amazingly—potatoes. You couldn't put potatoes on the grill raw—that was where he'd made his mistake before. But if you microwaved them, let them cool a bit, and then sliced them, a little slather of oil and they could go on the grill with some thickly sliced onions and the whole meal was right there on the fire.

In his basket were the items for tonight's grill and he thought, what if he added some other things, that was what a mixed grill was, wasn't it? But what to add? Shrimp would be good but wouldn't it fall through the grill? As he pondered this, he bumped baskets with his neighbor, Sophie Gold. He knew she was a regular visitor to his kitchen and he was grateful for all the goodies she constantly brought over for the kids because they needed that sense of security.

"Dr. M!" she said excitedly, "How are you? I haven't seen you in a while."

He smiled at her with genuine appreciation. "I can't apologize enough," he said. "I've been meaning to knock on your door, bring you some wine or at least some ice cream. You've been so wonderful to bring so many delicious goodies over. Candy says she's adopted you."

Mrs. G laughed, "Well, we adopted each other. And you know I love to cook. Just don't want Bert eating every bite I cook, wonky ticker. Trying to keep the old man around a little longer. Fifty years you know — in three months."

Bill sighed and looked at Mrs. G, "Fifty years. A whole lifetime. That's a lot of memories, wonderful memories for sure. I expected...."

Sophie patted Bill on the arm, "I know you did, I know. We all did. Listen — why don't you come over tonight and we'll have dinner together instead of me slipping over to drop off stuff so Chrissy doesn't starve those kids." She gulped, thought better of what she'd just said, not wanting to be too critical, then added, "Though I know she's been better lately."

"No, you know what — it's about time you came over and I fed you. I'm a cook now — and I'm making a mixed grill. Steaks and veg and what else is the mixed part is what I'm trying to figure out." He laughed as Sophie smiled at him as a mom would do at a slow child.

"Depends on the size of the grill," she said. "You can add chicken, sausages, nice fat asparagus, shrimp on skewers, anything really. You can do burgers, but with steak, it's nice to have a different meat — see — that's why it's mixed. But don't worry about dessert. I baked a couple pies earlier today."

Bill walked and Sophie strolled alongside him and they talked and laughed and tossed items in their respective baskets. Later Bill produced an acceptably good dinner, which the Golds proclaimed the best dinner ever and everyone enjoyed sitting together outside in the yard at the comfortable garden table.

Candy climbed into Sophie's lap after eating and said, "You know I'm really sorry, Mrs. G."

Sophie laughed and asked, "What are you sorry for, Cutie?"

"That you don't have children of course. It's so sad for you." Then she smiled mischievously and said, "But good for me," burrowing down against that warm and cozy lap.

"What?" said Bert. "Suddenly we got no kids? Nobody told me that."

Sophie laughed at her husband, thinking of the car they'd just bought for their granddaughter and said, "We have kids, they're just grown up like your daddy. And grandkids, older than you."

"But where are all these people?" asked Candy. "How come I never met them?"

"They live in San Francisco," said Bert. "But Gigi, the baby, she might be moving back here soon."

"But aren't you too old to have a baby? And how can she live where was it again with nobody to change her diapers?" asked Candy.

Bert laughed. "She's the youngest and still our baby but she's actually what, thirty seven?"

"Thirty nine," said Sophie. "She's a fantastic architect. Divorced about a year. She lives in San Francisco, Candy."

Will raised his thumb and pointed up so Candy would know where that was.

"Heaven?" Candy asked.

"San Francisco, dummy," said Will, "North of here. Up the freeway. Not heaven."

"Speaking of North of here," said Bert.

"Somebody's bedtime," said Sophie.

"No!" protested Candy, "I'm not ready to go to bed."

Sophie laughed. "I meant him, not you," she said, putting her hand on her husband's arm.

It had been a pleasant evening. Bill enjoyed entertaining, and never realized he could do it on his own. He didn't mind the cooking or the cleaning up after and he liked the company. They would do that again.

Once the dishes were done and the kids were tucked in, he sat in bed, reading a medical journal and relaxing. Then Chrissy blew into the bedroom like a storm cloud and she slammed — and locked — the door. Before he could even ask her what was wrong, she had tossed off her clothes and dropped them on the floor where she stood and then she was in bed astride him, maneuvering him into something that passed for sex — assuming they were two people in the military or the boxing ring.

She sat astride him, rising and falling, pumping and bouncing as though it were a timed competition. Her arms tightly wrapped around his back she moved at about the speed of a rabbit. "Do it. Do it. Do it more," she said, although she was doing most of the work and Bill was a passenger. "Harder, do it harder," forcing Bill to clench up with vigor, causing her thighs to slap down against his. "Push," she commanded, "Yes, push up. Up! Up! More!"

Bill closed his eyes and clung to Chrissy, moving in rhythm, and contemplated whether this would lead to orgasm or injury.

"Yes!" she shouted, "You got it! Right!"

More relieved than sated, Bill watched as she fell off of him and lay limply, her back to him, the covers pulled up around her. He slid over to spoon and cuddle, but her breath was too regular, and now and then a tiny snore came from her — she was already asleep.

Bill sighed and reached for his robe, then padded softly into the kitchen where he poured a glass of milk and opened a box of Malomars, which he ate silently, not even noticing that they were much smaller in size than the last box he'd bought.

Angie struggled with a weighty issue. She paced the floor of her now-empty deli, everything around her gleaming clean and ready for tomorrow. Still in the food case sat today's food, which would be emptied and donated or tossed. But the question was, should she listen to Dr. Masters' suggestion, which she feared. One bite led to two in her experience and two led to two hundred. Her inclination was to walk out the door and avoid this line of thought altogether. It was too easy just to say let's try it, let's check out all this amazing food that she'd been creating for so long, which other people got to enjoy daily and she got to enjoy never.

Then her face softened, her eyes brightened, and her heart quickened a pace. There was Kevin, the man of her dreams, her destiny, the person she was certain would become her future. And what had he told her. What *had* he told her? Didn't it seem as though Kevin were suggesting that she should seduce Dr. Masters? No, surely not. A person as honorable as Kevin would never connive and manipulate his partner in that manner. He clearly had been stressed. Who knew what was going on in his horrific marriage? Things like that took their toll on people, Angie was sure of that. But she did know that he had said trust Dr. Masters, or had he said get on his good side? But why? What would that serve? She was his patient not his employee. Maybe it would help Kevin in some way. But wasn't Kevin his partner, his equal? Why was he so afraid of Dr. Masters—or did he think Masters would tell on them, tell his wife, and then get him in trouble before he was ready to leave her? Messy divorces cost a lot more money, Angie knew that.

Yet maybe it made sense. She had eaten very little all day, so even if she tasted, perhaps tomorrow she could shore up her resolve, redouble her efforts, take the day off from the deli if necessary. But what if this were the slippery slope, the thing that would suck her back into the abyss of fat, just as it had done so many times before?

Angie sighed and she paced, walking back and forth to the display case, opening it once or twice, even taking a platter out and then returning it to the case. What a vexing situation. Finally, with a deep breath and the desperate hope that this wouldn't be the end of her slim self, she made herself a plate, one bite of each item in the case. At last, she would taste her food.

Tempted to stand at the case and just eat, she decided instead to set a place for herself at a table. It was an occasion, a special event, one she hopefully would not be repeating again for a very long time.

So there she sat, the plate before her, cutting edge, revolutionary cuisine ready for her to sample. She lifted the fork and took a bite, her face alight with both positive expectation and fear of being unable to stop herself. What if it was so fantastically delicious she couldn't stop? What if she grazed through the entire display case? Angie chewed slowly as she'd recently learned to do. She let the food move around against her taste buds. She chewed some more. And some more. And then she gulped. The expression on her face turned from glorious expectation mixed with fear of future addiction to unbelievable horror. But no, it couldn't be.

More bites followed. Bite after bite. Soon she began cutting her one-bite portions into half bites and small slivers. It didn't take long for her to register the same expression that Bill and Laura had endeavored to conceal.

"Oh my God!" she exclaimed. She felt like heaving the plate against a wall, but a knock on the door distracted her.

It was Ben. Angie rose, opened the door and in he came, opening his arms for a hug. She hugged him back rather distractedly then pulled away, unaware that he was still hugging. He stumbled a bit, then reached in toward her hoping to kiss her at last, but she turned her cheek to accept what was assumed to be a friendly kiss, which devolved into an awkward face to mouth bump. Ben blushed, once again foiled in his efforts, but of course Angie didn't notice at all, so distracted was she.

"My food sucks! Jesus this stuff is inedible."

She looked so upset that Ben tried immediately to help her. "No, you're a fantastic chef. Don't be silly. You're the best cook I ever met."

"Cutting edge cuisine, my ass."

"I love that spaghetti Bolognese you used to make."

Angie reached for the plate, removing it from the table, and started walking back toward the kitchen, but then something opened inside her and she turned toward Ben, her eyes wide. "I must have figured if I was giving up food then why make it wonderful for everyone else — why let them have pleasure while I was suffering."

Ben smiled at her, impressed with her insight.

"I know caramel doesn't belong inside meatballs," she said, her voice growing more excited, "And I transferred my anger at my dad into this cutting edge crap — making shitty food to punish people who were allowed to indulge." Angie paused a moment, still thinking. "How about that! He wasn't a quack." Angie smiled at Ben then and said, "Come on, I'm gonna make you some good food."

In short order Ben and Angie sat opposite each other eating plates of spaghetti with nice salads on the side. Ben ate happily and smiled at Angie. She was so wonderful. "Remember that scene in *Lady and the Tramp*?" he asked.

"Where all the dogs are depressed and locked up?" she replied, pausing for a moment to think about Ben. "Ahh, you're so sweet to worry about me. I'm fine, though. Really." She reached out and squeezed his hand, not noticing the disappointment that flickered across his face.

Kevin enjoyed driving along the serpentine curves of Sunset Boulevard in the evening. As long as he stayed west of the Sunset Strip, traffic was light and he could just relax and appreciate the excellent way his car handled.

At a conveniently discrete distance behind the Porsche, Butch and Wimp drove along, Kevin's frequent, mostly unnoticed shadow. Wimp had been worrying and fretting and attempting to get Butch to give up this quest. Butch turned to Wimp and said with assurance, "Not this time we won't. Watch this! I'm gonna lead this horse to water and then run him off the road." Her foot pressed down on the gas and the car sped forward, coming closer and closer to the Porsche.

Kevin turned around as a black SUV came so close to him it was practically riding on his bumper. Did he know that car? "What the devil," he muttered. He pressed down on the gas, speeding forward, determined to shake this insane driver. He sped up, changed lanes, craned his neck and squinted into the rearview mirror but couldn't see who was driving the car.

Closer and closer to Kevin's bumper Butch drove, almost grazing him, then backing off slightly with a chortle while beside her Wimp gulped and grasped the sides of his seat. "We're gonna crash into him, be careful," he said, terrified.

"Oh there's gonna be a crash all right, but it's not us who's crashing, it's the sound of his mean little mind exploding." Butch sped up once again and whizzed so close to Kevin's Porsche that he was forced almost to the side of the road. Feeling a surge of power, Butch sped up even more, ignoring the shrieks coming from the passenger seat. They were almost neck and neck in one lane. It was as good as a scene in a movie and she shivered a bit from the thrill of it all.

"Stop it, please," begged Wimp.

Looking all around him, Kevin spotted the entrance to the 405 freeway ahead of him on the other side of Sunset. Just as the maniac slowed a bit, he had his chance. He turned the wheel, crossed within inches of the several cars heading east on Sunset and blazed down the incline onto the freeway. He'd eluded them, well perhaps he had.

His heart was pounding but Kevin sensed all would be fine.

And then the sirens went off. Cops! Finally they would haul this psycho off to jail. The lights began swirling directly behind him and Kevin was forced to pull off to the side of the freeway. What in blazes! The cop hadn't been chasing the SUV at all.

Kevin glared at a cop so young he looked like he should have been tucked in on a school night, resting up for a test in long division in the morning. He launched into the detailed story of his near death experience but the cop looked at him without the slightest degree of believability. His face showed no expression at all. Then he said, "You can't pull across lanes of traffic and race onto the freeway like that. It's dangerous."

"Dangerous," said Kevin incredulously, "Didn't you hear what I just said? I wasn't planning to take the 405. I had to veer off the road because some maniac was chasing me. I would have ended up in a ditch between here and Sepulveda if I didn't. Black SUV—didn't you see them? They almost crashed into my bumper several times."

"You careened right in front of me," said the cop, with determination.

"So you had a perfect view of that SUV—very distinctive Honda CR-V I think. I'm sure I've seen them before too. They tried to run me off the road. It was deliberate too. I'm sure of it."

"Distinctive?" asked the cop with a knowing glance, "That's like the most common car on the road. If you're gonna make up an assailant at least be creative."

"I'll have you know I'm a doctor, not some crazy liar. If you did your job at all you would have seen what just happened here. And you'd be hauling them off to jail. That would be you — doing your job."

"This is me doing my job," said the cop, handing Kevin back his license and a ticket.

Kevin glared at the cop. "How could you see me and not see them?" he asked repeatedly. Then he snatched the ticket and muttered, "Tax dollars at work."

"Watch your speed," said the cop, "And signal then change lanes slowly."

"Asshole," muttered Kevin, as he drove away, glancing to left and right, looking for that black vehicle, which by now was probably out there running over a toddler. And then this underage moron in blue could give the undertaker a summons.

SEVEN

Bill and Laura were in the final stages of party planning. They strolled, side by side, through a cavernous party rental place, from which anything from the most elegant china to paper plates could be rented or bought. There were aisles filled with a massive variety of different patterns of china, or stemware, or table linens in every possible color. There were platters. Even little hibachis. And there were tables and chairs of all sizes, shapes, and designs. There were shimmery little slipcovers to go over the chairs. It was a world of gossamer fantasy if you were a bride and the bowels of hell if you were a groom.

Every now and then Laura would hold something up, a plate, a glass, a tablecloth, and Bill invariably nodded. He might have felt clueless about tasks of this nature had he actually been focusing on the design aspects or the social aspects. Instead he was talking about the past and the future.

"I worked so hard at the beginning. I was never there. JoEllen used to say I was missing stuff at home. But what was I going to do? I couldn't sit home and be a poet, could I? If you're going to be a doctor, you're going to work hard, but your family benefits and eventually there's more time." Bill sighed heavily. "How was I to know there wasn't going to be that time?"

Laura shook her head and rested her hand gently on Bill's shoulder. "Of course you couldn't know. Nobody can fast forward through to the end of their lives like it's a novel where you can read the last page. Nobody can do that and go back to the beginning and change things. You just do your best as you go along."

"This time I said, okay, I'm going to be there and pay attention. I'm doing nothing wrong, everything just right. That's why this party. I thought it would mean something."

"You can't make up with Chrissy for what you missed with JoEllen, you know. It doesn't work that way."

Bill sighed. "Nope. I know. Doesn't mean I shouldn't try to do better."

Laura stopped walking, stopped browsing, and just looked at Bill. "I don't think she was ever really mad at you. Or even that she thought you weren't doing your best. She always knew what kind of man you were."

Bill felt a cloud of what passed for relief cross his heart. It wasn't so much that he lived with the burden of JoEllen's anger, for she had never been an angry person. She was a joyful person, and he loved that about her. But so often he stopped to consider the past, to think of what he might have done differently, done better. It was as though he yearned to rewrite the past so that all the time subsumed in the parenthesis of his marriage, that part of his life that now was over, due to no fault of his own, nor of his own choosing, so that that part could be made better, that every second of it could be shining and perfect and without the most minor of flaws and in so doing could be bigger and not be what it ultimately would become should he live a reasonably long life, the tiny period of time in which he was happily married to the great love of his life.

Bill knew that he had not been a bad husband. He knew that what he missed was the continuity of the past within the present, and in missing that present, he yearned for those moments in the past when so casually he had been elsewhere. He had been making notes on a patient's chart, not seeing a movie with JoEllen. He had been reordering supplies or having a drink with a drug rep, instead of having an extra hour with his family. Was he someone who took it all for granted at the time? That was his fear. He had been too cavalier, and he hadn't cherished what was soon wrenched from him. Maybe if he had done so with more urgency, maybe, no it was silly. He wasn't a superstitious fool. He did not believe that he had somehow brought about the demise of his happy life through some kind of lack of appreciation. He hadn't been unappreciative; he'd just worked and lived his life in a normal manner. Nor had he been uncaring or unfaithful. JoEllen and the kids were always in his heart like a family portrait that hung within its walls. He just wished he still had now what he had then. And whatever he could do to make it so, he would do.

"I didn't think she was mad at me. Just that, just that, you know, all gone too soon."

"I know. Of course I know. Nothing's worse than a premature ending."

Bill nodded. Premature. Exactly.

"JoEllen said I should ditch Kevin. After that incident," Laura said. "I just can't see myself twice divorced. It would be shameful. And he swore he'd...."

Bill snorted. "Nobody would count that two day marriage you had in college. You were drunk at the time."

A wry look of disgust shone in Laura's eyes. "Too bad I'm not drunk through this one."

"Relationships are hard. To know that you're on the right track...that the feelings are right...lasting. But how do you know that? How do you really know?"

Laura smiled softly. "I think you know. You knew before. We had one date and then you met my roommate and it was like you were thunderstruck. You couldn't see anyone else ever again. There could have been a naked marching band in the room and you wouldn't have noticed."

"Are we talking good looking bandoliers or uggos?" Bill asked, laughing.

"The Apocalypse could have started and you would have been mooning over JoEllen."

"Going to the library was a date?" Bill asked.

Laura laughed. "You see — when you were with JoEllen you didn't not know it was a date."

"Well in the grand scheme of things, what I didn't know was a lot, but that I knew. But it's not like there are JoEllens standing on every corner. She was a once in a lifetime thing. And now...."

"There's Chrissy. And a party," said Laura, her voice as neutral as she could make it.

Bill nodded.

Chrissy kept thinking about that saying, when a door closes a window opens. What this meant she wasn't entirely sure because most people didn't really walk through a window, though of course anyone could climb out one, assuming it wasn't on a high floor. Air could come in, and that was a good thing because nobody would want to smother in a closed in room. But what did all that have to do with her situation? She was unsure but on some level, she felt this saying summed it up. She had found her niche. Maybe that was the actual saying that described it? She was still unsure, but at least there seemed to be some hope for her future, and Chrissy felt gratified that she had posted that ad on Craig's List as a personal trainer. Maybe the saying was that when a window closed a door opened? That way you could fit a treadmill through the door.

Carefully swallowing her third set of over the counter diet pills and herbal diet aids for the day, Chrissy repeated her new mantra, *everything is great, everything is good, everything is wonderful, and I am thin.* Fingering the gleaming stop watch around her neck, she bound up the stairs to her new clients' home gym. She was here, she was ready, she was great. These people were serious about working out and about getting into the best shape of their lives. To Chrissy this sounded so good that her first words into the door were, "I'm here and ready to get you into the best shape of your lives."

Lisa, a pretty blond trophy wife, was Chrissy's age and it was clear she knew what was important. She looked as though she hadn't had a bite of candy since Halloween in the third grade. Her husband Norm was ten years older and another matter. He looked almost fit, well, formerly fit. He was starting to get complacent and that was what Chrissy was here to reverse.

Chrissy settled Lisa onto a rowing machine and Norm onto the treadmill then walked between them offering motivation and changing the settings as necessary. "That's it, both of you," Chrissy said in her most encouraging manner. She'd decided that rather than letting that horrible incident at the weight loss center become her Waterbug, she was going to climb out of the drain and make a success of her life. Wait—Waterbug—wasn't that in France—that short guy with the funny big hat? Chrissy shook her head. Too often lately her mind became distracted. Well who was in charge here, her mind or her? As long as it wasn't her stomach, she was ahead of the game. Turning her focus back to her clients, Chrissy said confidently, "I want to see some sweat here. This is no dainty workout. You're gonna give me your all minus, hmmm, fifteen percent." Percents were so complicated, weren't they, but that's the way people always said it, all minus some percent, at least it was like that in the stores when stuff was on sale.

Norm, an accountant, looked at her quizzically, so she adjusted his treadmill, and as Lisa watched, clearly concerned, the incline increased and increased to an angle so steep Norm might as well have been attempting to scale the Himalayas. He struggled valiantly, holding tightly to the side rails of the machine as Lisa, concerned for his safety, rowed even more energetically.

Norm's breath began to come a bit more raggedly, his pace less smooth, and as he reached for the controls to lower the incline, Chrissy slapped his hand away. "Don't you even think about it, Norm!" she said sternly, "You have a year of beer and pretzels to work off. Another year of champagne and caviar. Golf? Golf! Don't even get me started on that b-s. Move it!"

Lisa rowed effortlessly, just as she did several hours a day every day while Norm was at work, but her eyes remained on her husband as his pace grew more and more unsteady. "Say, Chrissy," she said with concern, "You should adjust that."

Chrissy nodded with fervor. "You're right. He's not giving that fifteen percent is he." And she upped the incline to its max and upped the speed as well. "C'mon Norm, show us what you're made of. You can do it, buddy. This will pay off in the bedroom, I can tell you that."

Norm looked at Chrissy then at his wife, then up in the air for a moment, picturing how this pace would be received in the bedroom. Not even the vacuum whirred this fast. He attempted to move faster, the sweat flying in all directions in a manner he could only consider gross. No matter how he clung to the rails at the side, the machine was going too fast for him, and his head began to swim. His face grew flushed and he felt a little woozy. He wanted to yell help, but couldn't get his breath regulated enough to speak, wanted to turn the machine off but was afraid to let loose of the rail, even with one hand.

Gasping, Norm reached for a water bottle, planning to douse his face with it, but it slid through his fingers, bouncing along the racing treadmill and onto the floor behind it. He felt something inside of him clench then, and his eyes rolled back into his head, his hands let go and the machine flung him off too, as his hand reached for his chest.

In the background he could hear Lisa yelling his name and Chrissy yelling, "Norm, get up immediately. No faking." Then it all went black.

Chrissy was truly appalled when the paramedics arrived within minutes, all sorts of medical gadgets at the ready to shock Norm awake. How could anyone let himself get so out of shape, she wondered. In short order they'd revived him, but were still loading him on a stretcher and carrying him out to the ambulance. Lisa didn't even finish her session. She clung to her husband's hand and climbed into the ambulance beside him, shaking a fist at Chrissy, who was clearly the victim in all of this — she hadn't even been paid.

Chrissy wondered should she wait for Lisa to return, but hospitals were pretty slow so that would be hours. She sat in her car, annoyed and frustrated. Now and then she leaned forward and banged her head on the wheel, but wow that hurt and it didn't seem to clear her head at all.

There was no way Kevin was going to let that psycho get the best of him — nobody got the best of Kevin. And although he had the sense that he should avoid Sunset Boulevard for a while, he was damned if he would — fear was never going to be his co-pilot. He was a tax paying American and a damned fine driver. And besides his house was right off Sunset, so he had to get home.

He drove reasonably, the Porsche handling the seductive curves like a bustier on a bimbo. Kevin loved this image and as he drove, he laughed, picturing many sets of breasts inside many bustiers. But then it happened — there they were. Again. Frantically he thought about what to do and then epiphany struck — he could spin his car around and chase them — put the fear of God into them. How would they feel when he was on their tail?

But the determined black car was right on his rear bumper and he still couldn't see who was behind the wheel. The setting sun was in his eyes, shining too brightly to make out any image of the other driver. But so what. Even if he could see who it was, what good would that do?

Maybe he should instigate a cataclysmic showdown. As the car came closer and closer, he should slam on his brakes, let them crash into him. He had excellent belts and bags and would be fine. And a psycho like that probably wasn't wearing seatbelts at all. Maybe they'd shoot through the winshield and be launched into space, or better yet into the path of an oncoming vehicle.

Kevin kept driving, the other car on his tail, and just as they were about to crash, he slammed on the brakes, but the other car pulled out into the middle lane and a third car screeched to a stop behind him then smoothly pulled around him, making an obscene gesture, like he was some kind of menace.

And then, again, the cop lights went off. Surely this time the cop would have seen what happened. Kevin, at first relieved, opened his window to face the same barely pubescent cop, who by rights should have taken after his assailant.

"You again," said Kevin with disgust. "You didn't see that fucking black SUV again? They've been trying to run me off the road for days."

"Watch the language, doctor," said the cop mellowly.

"Language," squawked Kevin, "Language? Language? That's what you think is important now? Never mind that someone has been tailgating me, deliberately trying to run me off the road for days? But no you're worried about a language violation?"

"I saw the red VW you nearly caused to crash into you by coming to an abrupt stop. Make you feel any better?"

"Oh my freaking God!" shouted Kevin. "The other car. The *other* car. The black SUV. The black SUV that tried to run me off the road. The black SUV that veered around me before the VW. Are you telling me you didn't see that?"

The officer handed Kevin another ticket and said "I'm telling you this. Clean up your act. Learn to drive."

Kevin snatched the ticket out of the cop's hand and drove away, yelling "Donut eating asshole," out of his window.

Bill and Angie sat congenially at one of the small tables in her deli. There were several plates of food ready to be tasted and approved. Briefly they laughed as they talked.

"And I actually told Kevin—Dr. Flicker—I thought you were a quack," said Angie with a big smile, which Bill returned. "You really helped," she went on, beginning to babble, a glazed look muddling her eyes. She'd concluded Bill was a hero, and the look of adoration crossing her face was unmistakable. "You're a real healer, very talented, quite amazing. I'm so impressed, I just can't say. Well I am saying, I'm saying it right now, right out loud. Nobody has ever...."

Bill gave her hand a quick, fatherly squeeze. He was glad she was doing well. Angie immediately reached out and pressed her other hand on top of his, rubbing it seductively.

As Bill removed his hands, he said, "Stop right now. Think about what you're feeling and why."

"Oh my God!" exclaimed Angie, "You're correct again. And you saw it right away."

At that moment Laura arrived and Bill rose to hug her, and pulled out a chair so she could sit and approve the last bit of food for the menu. They each took some bites, nodding happily and smiling at Angie, who beamed.

Chrissy had taken refuge in the one place where her life always made sense — Zero Tolerance. Happily noting the collection of air purifiers placed in virtually every corner, prominently placed in fact, Chrissy was determined to work off all her aggravation and frustration. Spinning. It was her secret source of serenity. Her legs pumped speedily and smoothly and she took several deep, cleansing breaths. And then her eyes snapped open and her head started to pound again. Her jaw clenched.

"Dammit," she said rather loudly, "I still smell it. Doesn't reek any more but I smell it." She looked up quizzically to those around her who had suddenly turned to stare in her direction. Instead of wondering why she was speaking out loud to no one, maybe they should have been wondering what to do about this invasion of odor. She waved her arm toward the door as though that gesture made it all clear, but by then everyone had resumed working out and focusing only on themselves.

Gathering up her stuff without even showering, Chrissy was determined to deal with this smelly situation. The gym had done their part. There was nowhere left to install an additional air purifier. Short of wearing an oxygen mask, Chrissy would have to confront this horrid deli and stop the intrusion into her sanctum of serenity.

She strode down the street with confidence and purpose—nobody could stop her now. Except something did stop her, Bill and Laura, on one of their dates, inside the deli, laughing and smiling. She could even hear their voices if she strained.

"So we're all set," said Laura happily. That smug bitch.

Bill smiled at Laura like she was the only woman on earth. When had he last smiled at Chrissy that way? Even his lovemaking had grown sluggish. "I can't wait for the weekend," he said.

"It's gonna be fantastic in every way," said the deli girl improbably. "Food and fun."

Chrissy felt a dagger plunge deeply into her heart. This was no treadmill injury—this was the real thing—piercing emotional pain. She stood there, pressed against the side of the building to remain unseen, but twisting and squirming in agony, attempting to decide what steps she should take. Should she maybe just stride in there, young, aglow and alive and confront Bill? She wrapped her arms around her head, trying to squeeze an answer out of her brain.

But then there were Bill and Laura, calmly walking down the street away from the deli as though nothing at all were wrong. Where was the guilt—that was what Chrissy wanted to know. The man had no shame and she was hitching her wagon to his horse? What had she been thinking? But really it all made sense. Look at the way he so cavalierly ate ice cream and sandwiches and virtually everything she couldn't, right in front of her. Look at the way, night after night, he came home with bags full of food. Look at how every night he was either cooking or wanting to go out to eat. The man was a, was a, what was the word for someone who cared about nothing but food? Son of a bitch, that was the word. No wonder he constantly refused to get her the Koush Koush, a drug she desperately needed. Then she'd be thin and he'd be a big fat burger slurping cow. Chrissy was seething and grew more livid the longer she pondered this betrayal.

Gulping, Chrissy strode into the deli like a boxer about to climb into the ring and pulverize a long-time nemesis. She glared at the deli girl with absolute hatred and rage. Her words poured out in an unstoppable stream, "We can smell this place inside the gym. Nobody can work out because of you. You're going to have to keep the kitchen door and windows tightly shut. It's the only decent thing to do."

Angie examined the clearly hysterical girl in front of her, considering what reply would make most sense, but ultimately all she could do was just be honest and reasonable and hope that she'd calm down a little. "It gets hot in there. I have assistants. They need to breathe."

"They're kitchen workers," said Chrissy, becoming more and more distraught, "They're used to the heat." Then she burst into tears and cried with so much rage and force that Angie was afraid she'd bring on a stroke. "My whole life is falling apart," Chrissy bleated, "I don't need this shit now too."

"Oh you poor thing," said Angie sympathetically. "Come and sit down and have a cookie."

Chrissy's voice cracked and she croaked, "A cookie! A cookie? What are you — Satan?"

Angie had calmed Chrissy down a little and had got her seated at a table, drinking mineral water and eating an undressed salad. As they shared a plate of colorful sorbets, Angie spoke calmly, "It's scary to think someone you love might be leaving you, but maybe it's all in your imagination. You gotta have faith sometimes. There's this doctor I'm in love with. He's taken but I know that's ending. He all but told me we're gonna be together. I'm seeing him this weekend."

Chrissy gasped, leapt from the table, knocking over her chair, and ran out of the deli as Angie watched in surprise.

Ben felt that in a way it was a good thing his most deeply disturbed client called him before he was due to go on a date. At least the hour he'd spend calming her down would help take his mind off the fact that he'd agreed to capitulate. Clint had been right and his offer to set Ben up with a nice sweet girl made sense. It was clear that to Angie he was completely invisible. He'd loved her virtually all his life and she'd never even noticed. To her he was a friend, and for all he knew, someone she considered a gay best friend, not the man she was meant to spend a lifetime loving. It was tragic, but it would have been more tragic if he had lingered in limbo, loving Angie and drifting all alone toward what would ultimately become senility. So he said yes, and this nice sweet girl was coming over and then they were going to dinner. Clint was out, allowing Ben to have the place to himself.

But at the moment he was busy placating this client who'd initially come to him to work through some of her food issues and by now had sunk into paranoia so deep that Ben wondered would he have to refer her to a psychiatrist who could install her in a hospital on twenty-four hour watch. She didn't seem suicidal, although she sounded a little homicidal, but Ben was pretty sure it was mostly rhetoric. He didn't stop to question whether he in any way was to blame for someone who at the beginning of therapy had seemed normal, a bit addicted to sweets, but coherent, and now sounded like a raving lunatic. Sometimes it took a while for the issues under the surface to emerge.

Chrissy was ranting, and this was the third time she had said the very same thing, her words punctuated with sniffles and deep sobs, "Him and two other women. And one is…." Here she took a big slobbering sob and continued, "Younger. And there's…" and here her voice grew more enraged, more filled with disgust, as she gasped, "Food play too." She stopped for a moment, just to sob, and then continued, "A fucking orgy." Then from her mouth came several guttural sounds as though she were bringing up a hair ball, and she said, enraged, "I'm going to get him. I'd like to shove a Malomar in his mouth and tape it shut. He'd love that though. Not as though there isn't one in his mouth every minute of the day. Um Malomars I mean, not tape."

"Okay now Chrissy, I want you to listen to me," said Ben calmly, also repeating himself for the third time. "Just focus on what I'm saying. Take a deep breath. C'mon now, let's get you breathing again."

"I'm breathing. You can hear me breathing, can't you? I'd be dead otherwise, wouldn't I? Most people have to breathe, don't they?" Then Chrissy took several slobbery breaths through her nose, trying to clear it, then Ben heard her blow her nose a couple of times with very loud honks.

"Good job," he said calmly. "You're already sounding better. But the thing is this — you're mad at your boyfriend, but you've never once had a conversation with him about this supposed affair, am I right?"

Chrissy began weeping again, and Ben could hear her muffled sobs, and he knew she was trying to conceal them from him.

"It's ok to cry, Chrissy, if you're feeling sad, let it out. I know you're upset. I'm just trying to say that sometimes a conversation makes a big difference when it comes to impressions we have about other people. Then they can answer for themselves."

"What's he gonna say? He has to date other women so he has someone to stuff his face with? Every time I see them they're eating. She's a big honking woman, too. Like a size six, maybe an eight. She's a plus sized woman. He's into the fatties. Oh my God, that's it. That's *it!* I never put it together before. I was a little plump when we met, maybe as big as a size four. He likes fat women. That's why he won't get me the Koush Koush."

"Didn't you say he's a physician?" asked Ben, "A diet doctor," thinking about Angie and this quack she was always talking about. But no, this one's name was Bill, not Kevin.

"Yes!" snorted Chrissy. "Well, I'm going to give him some of his own medicine. Ha!"

Ben was concerned enough to ask, "You're not planning to drug his food or anything, right?"

"If I had the freaking Koush Koush you can bet I'd dose him with it, then maybe we'd be compatible again, a normal dieting couple in Beverly Hills. And nobody would have to fly off to India, would they?" Chrissy laughed then and said, "Gotta run. Thank you so much. Talk to you soon. I'll let you know what happens. Don't worry, Ben, I'm not planning to feed him an arsenic soufflé. I don't know how to make a soufflé."

Before Ben could keep her on the line long enough to be certain he didn't have to call the authorities, she was gone, leaving him wondering just what she was planning. At least she sounded calmer at the end of the call than at the beginning, so that was hopeful. And then the doorbell rang and he was face to face with the nice, sweet girl.

Admittedly Clint hadn't seen Colette since he broke her older sister's heart in high school, and at that time she was what—twelve—but his description of her as a sweet little girl with a smile that lit up the room was still apt, but of course he'd seen a recent picture on Facebook. Colette walked in wearing a white sun dress made of some sort of fabric with little stitched holes that laced up the front with a pink ribbon and had a teeny pink belt. She looked like she'd just come from a garden party, but to Ben that was great. For a while he'd been nervous, expecting someone who dressed like an escapee from a hooker emporium, but at least it wouldn't feel too scary escorting this nice young woman on a date.

"Where's Clint?" she said a bit too breathlessly.

"Hmm, I'm not exactly sure," said Ben honestly. "Can I offer you some wine before we leave for dinner?"

Colette nodded, and sat down on the couch. "Clint will be here soon, won't he?" she asked.

"Gosh, I doubt it," said Ben, walking in from the kitchen with a tray he'd prepared with cheese and crackers and a nice bottle of wine.

"Oh so this is supposed to be a real date?" Colette asked.

"Oh," sighed Ben, suddenly aware of what was going on. "What did Clint tell you, anyway?"

"He said he had a nice guy for me to meet. But somehow I thought... oh I'm silly, you'll hate me, I thought...."

"Clint, you thought Clint," Ben said.

"Well, you know how it is when you have the feeling that someone is just meant for you? I was just this kid in school and Clint was dating my sister, and you could just see no way were they suited for each other, and I had this sense, this little feeling, but I was just this kid, and everyone laughed, said he was like a dress up crush, like when you play dress up and pretend you're married, and he was just the pretend guy. But I always thought, no, he's the guy."

Ben smiled, handing a cracker with some cheese to Colette and swallowing one himself. "Oh I know a thing or two about that feeling. To tell the truth this evening was supposed to be the antidote for that feeling."

Colette smiled and nodded. "Is he seeing anyone?"

Ben looked sympathetic but was honest, "He's always seeing someone, in fact usually everyone."

"He has lots of friends on Facebook. Like twelve hundred women and five guys."

"It takes six guys to play basketball," said Ben. "Tell you what. You're here, it's dinner time, I can order some Chinese, or we can go out and come back. Eventually he'll be back and you two can sit and catch up. At least it will feel natural that way, not forced. And you look so pretty."

Colette smiled. "You are nice. It's too bad I didn't meet you first."

Ben laughed. "I've been in love since third grade with this adorable brown haired girl."

"Tell me all about her," said Colette.

- EIGHT -

This was the day. Bill noted with satisfaction the red circle on today's calendar page. The party would soon begin and it would be a wonderful evening and they would be what he wanted—a happy family enjoying a celebration together. Chrissy would be surprised and would snap out of the crazy spell she'd been under. This would be the turning point in which everything went back to the way it was meant to be. Angie had worked really hard and he flipped through the pictures she'd just sent to his email. Everything was set up, and that giant banner saying "Happy Birthday, Chrissy," was an inspiration. She would be so thrilled, he just knew it.

He pressed a button on his speaker phone and reached to unzip the garment bag hanging on his closet door.

Laura answered on one ring, and in a goofy voice, said. "Party central."

Bill laughed. "Well, this is it. We're all set. I have pictures right here from Angie and it's all perfect. All that's missing is us."

"Hard to imagine she has no clue," said Laura, the irony not lost on her at all.

"None," said Bill. "She thinks it's an anti-smoking fund raiser. What time are you picking her up?"

"I've got the kids right here," said Laura, "And we were going to get her but Kevin called and said he could do it, so I said sure, great. So rare that he makes a thoughtful gesture."

"That's actually much better. We can all be there to yell surprise when she walks in with Kevin. See — things do have a way of working out."

"Will!" said Laura, "Will, no, don't do that. Oh geez. Bit of a spill — okay see you at the party."

Bill shrugged, knowing it was nothing serious, and began changing for the party. He pulled up the slacks of his tuxedo and twisted and turned. Had they always been this tight? He knew they hadn't. The jacket looked like he'd borrowed it from an organ grinder's monkey. He turned this way and that and gazed at himself sausaged into a tux that was more than a size too small. He shook his head and sighed. Then he opened his desk drawer and removed his stash of candy bars and tossed them into the trash. The joke was on him. Now he'd have to go home and change into a suit, assuming he had one that fit. Bill laughed at himself as he slipped back into his clothes, zipped the tux back into its bag and walked through the empty waiting room. At least there was still plenty of time.

Bill pulled into his driveway behind Kevin's Porsche just as Laura pulled in behind him and emerged from the car in a stunning evening gown. Bill pressed his hand to his heart, "Wow, lady, you're a knockout."

Laura smiled and said, "Will needs another shirt. Balancing cans of soda on his head."

"Runs in the family," said Bill. "Tuxedo's way too tight. Malomars and candy bars. Physician heal thyself."

"Ahh no. You just haven't worn that tux in ages. Okay kids, let's get that shirt. We have a party to attend."

"C'mon let's go see my grandma. I want her to see me all dressed up," said Candy.

"Your grandma moved in next door?" asked Julie.

"Well, she's adopted, but yes," said Candy.

"She'll see you at the party," said Bill. But the kids were half way across the lawn by then. "Will, come back here, you need to change."

"It's okay," said Laura, "I'll grab a shirt and he can put it on in the car."

Bill unlocked the door and held it open for Laura and they both walked toward the back of the house, but it was only a moment before they stopped, listening to noises that should not have been coming from the bedroom. A familiar look of resignation crossed Laura's face while Bill's registered disbelief. It must be something else. He strode toward the bedroom with Laura behind him.

And there in Bill's bed sat Kevin and Chrissy, smoking. Both grabbed for the sheets as their respective partners entered the room. Bill stood looking at the couple, shaking his head sadly, as Laura grew enraged, almost more at the cigarettes than the obvious. "Screwing *and* smoking," she said, "A new low, even for you." Then Laura turned and walked out of the room.

Chrissy gazed at Bill with utter insolence, and in moving slightly, an emptied jar of fudge sauce tumbled out of the bed and onto the carpet. She looked down at the fudge then back up defiantly.

"Here's what's going to happen," said Bill with icy precision. "I'm going to a party to make excuses. Happy Birthday, Chrissy, by the way—surprise! When I get home you won't be here. And Monday," pointing at

Kevin, "When I get to work, you won't be there. The both of you can go to hell where you belong."

"I can't get all my stuff out of here tonight," asserted Chrissy, determined to stand up to Bill despite the look on his face. "Who do you think you are anyway, not like I don't know what's been going on with you and her." She pointed toward the door where Laura no longer stood as Bill just shook his head at her.

Kevin looked toward the doorway his wife had vacated and wondered only briefly what Chrissy was talking about, then returned his focus to the more important issue. "Why should I give up half a practice that's mine?" asked Kevin.

"I'll get moving men to deliver your exercise crap wherever you want. And I'll get a lawyer to split the practice. Both of you — get the hell out of my house. I'm calling the security company and they'll make sure you're out, stuff or no stuff."

Bill turned and strode out the door, grabbing a suit jacket from his closet. He walked outside and stood next to Laura by their cars, a hand on her arm to steady her. "I'm sorry you had to see that," he said.

"Which part," she asked, "The screwing, the smoking or the fudge?"

Bill shook his head, "What a couple of schnooks we are, huh. Thank God the kids weren't with us."

Laura nodded wryly. "So what do we do now? Call the caterer and cancel?"

"I hate to do that to her, she's so sensitive, she'll take it personally. Plus so many friends are probably already there. I'll just go, make up a lie, hope it ends early. If I stay here I might take a baseball bat to them."

"We're always stuck being the grownups," said Laura. "Should we just take one car?"

And that was what they did. According to Bill, Chrissy was sick and each time someone asked where she was, he made up a new, even creepier disease. As most of the people there were Bill's friends, not Chrissy's, nobody really minded her absence and they also didn't leave early. They had a good time and nobody noticed how subdued both Bill and Laura were.

Sophie and Bert were the last to leave because Mrs. G had wanted to stay and help, although no help was needed. Angie's crew was top notch and the party would have been a huge success under different circumstances. Sophie smiled toward the back, where the girls had conked out on some chairs. Will was riding the carousel, determined to set a record and each time he did another round, he shouted out the number.

"It was a lovely party, dear," said Sophie, although she could see something was wrong when she looked into Bill's eyes. "Need someone to listen?" she asked.

Bill smiled at her and made a gesture, his hand slicing across his throat and a squawky sound coming from his lips.

"Well, maybe it's for the best," she said, knowing instantly what he meant. "Want us to stick around a while?" Bert stood by her side, and although he was tired, he said nothing.

Bill hugged his neighbor and said, "Oh no, thanks though. We're leaving too in just a couple minutes."

"Okay then, it's up this hill to our car. If you want to stop by later, I'll be up for a while."

Bill smiled at Sophie and watched her and Bert go up the tall hill that led from the pier to the street. He didn't know if they'd parked on the pier itself, on the street, or in one of the nearby lots but it was a bit of a trek and he hoped they'd parked on the pier.

He gazed off into the distance, where a few feet away Laura had raced over to a young couple who were smoking. They peered into her eyes, growing more and more alarmed, not so much because of her message but because she was becoming so emotional that she sounded almost unhinged.

"Oh no, you're smoking. Please! Think about what you're doing. You could lose your life, lose each other. Everything would be over. Dead. I'm talking final here, final, end, no more, nothing more, completely over and dead."

Without a word, the couple turned and raced away, their pace becoming more rapid with each step. Laura observed them and began weeping, and she stumbled toward the carousel as Bill walked toward her and took her in his arms.

Her sobbing grew more pronounced, her breath ragged, her words coming in breathy gasps. "Control was all I wanted. I thought if I could make a difference, make them stop smoking, then at least I could feel I had a handle on something, was doing something, getting something right, something good." Then she laughed, sobbed some more, and sniffled, saying, "Fighting the devil."

Bill dabbed at her eyes with his handkerchief.

Laura sobbed and wheezed a bit, saying, "But there is no control. I should know that by now after all these years with Kevin."

"Ah honey," said Bill, cleaning up her streaky face with his handkerchief.

"Do you think I married him so I could face all this? Face that there's never any control? Face that there's no safety?" She took the handkerchief and mopped at her eyes then resumed sobbing. "If I could live with Kevin all these years, maybe I don't need as much control as I thought."

"Ahhhh, honey it's okay. You'll be okay. Come here." Bill wrapped his arms around Laura and held her tightly until the sobbing turned into an occasional sniffle. Then she dabbed her face again and blew her nose. They sat down together on a couple of chairs and just tried to breathe for a while.

"Are you going to leave him?" Bill asked.

"I don't know."

"The two divorce thing?"

"Maybe I'll just let him see me snuggling in bed a few times with the puppy. Drive him totally over the edge."

They both laughed as Laura continued, "Here I am sobbing all over you, and you're in the same boat I am."

Bill shrugged. "You know — I don't actually feel that bad. I keep waiting for it to sink in, but all I can think of is two things. First, JoEllen is dead. She's not coming back. And second, Chrissy is history. Thank God!" He stopped to think for a moment and realized he'd been right earlier — everything had changed tonight, just not in the way he'd expected but somehow it was all right. "You know — I gained fifteen pounds since she moved in."

They both laughed and Laura said, "Be glad it was you. If she'd gained weight from living with you, she probably would've hired a couple thugs to murder you."

"No kidding!" Bill smiled and shook his head then his voice grew softer, "So I guess I'm back to square one again. All alone."

"You're so much better off without her. She was just a diversion. Someone else will come along. You'll see. And you'll be happy again. In love again."

Bill looked into Laura's eyes and grew dazzled by what she was saying. Happy again. In love again. Compelling words. As if entranced, he reached over to kiss her, which she assumed was a peck on the cheek but as soon as she realized what he was about to do, Laura leapt up and stared at him, her hands on her hips.

"What are you doing?"

"I thought...you looked so...it seemed like...."

"Good God, Bill, you're doing it again—this time trying to plug me in for JoEllen. That's not right."

"No, wait, I don't think so." He reached for her again but she jumped back.

"For God's sake, are all you men the same?"

"But it's been so wonderful spending this time with you, and I felt, I felt...."

"Of course you've enjoyed it—all we do is talk about JoEllen. I'm like a conduit to her. And that's fine because we're friends. But why would I want to be with someone who just wants me to remember his wife with him. That's not love. Love is you see someone and you can't remember anyone else, not even JoEllen."

"Ah geez I'm sorry," said Bill.

"Forget it. That was one hell of a crappy party."

Bill laughed. "Yeah, let's get the kids and go home."

There was a benefit to infidelity despite the obvious, Kevin thought. The time he was spending mentally calculating the penance he'd have to pay, the gifts he'd have to buy, the promises he'd have to make in order to keep his wife in line, had completely taken his mind off the traveling circus of psychosis that driving along Sunset Boulevard had become. He almost laughed. How had he let himself become so paranoid? Just this afternoon he was peering to the left and to the right like a pony express driver deep in Indian country. Surely it was just some crazy coincidence. After all what had that teeny bopper in blue said—the car he was certain was after him was the most popular car on the road. Or the most popular SUV. Something like that. Come to think of it, he'd been through so much lately. He was in a precarious mental state because of this presumed harassment, and that might make sense to Bill when he went in to confront him about this rift between them. Yes, he'd have to kiss some hairy ass, do some genuflecting, make some threats too. He could hire a lawyer too, for sure he could threaten that. After all, Chrissy wasn't Bill's wife and the point could be made that Kevin's temporary insanity had saved Bill from a terrible fate—marriage. Bill was a reasonable man and Kevin could probably make him see it that way.

Or he could say it was Chrissy's fault. He was there just to do a good deed, to pick up his partner's girlfriend for a surprise party and how could he know she would force him to have sex with her? That was another kind of surprise, one he wasn't ready to defend against. In his state of hysteria, how could he be responsible for his actions? Kevin took a deep breath, and he realized he was starting to feel a lot better. Things were looking up. And then Kevin too looked up and there they were — again — almost neck and neck with him in a single lane. How did the cars not crash?

Something in Kevin snapped. He wasn't going to take this any longer. First his partner's girlfriend practically rapes him, his partner threatens him with shysters, his wife looks at him like he's garbage and now this — well somewhere he had to draw the line.

"Okay, motherfucker," he said, enraged, "See how you like it!" And he sped up, and wow did the Porsche respond like a dream — worth every penny he'd paid for it, and then, just like one of those steely race car drivers, he spun the car around and now he was the one chasing that demented asshole. "Take that, you piece of shit," he said with much satisfaction, although of course the windows were closed and nobody heard but him. Maybe he should open the window so they'd hear what he had to say — just before he ran them off the road. Yeah, justice at last. The chase continued with the hunter becoming the hunted or so it seemed in Kevin's imagination.

"The worm has turned," exclaimed Butch grimly, as her hands tightened on the steering wheel. She and Wimp exchanged one frantic glance.

Butch endeavored merely to stay ahead of the Porsche. This was emphatically not part of the plan. The cars sped along, a rare string of green lights allowing them to race forward, and Butch managed to keep from being rammed although the squealing of wheels caused Wimp to cover his ears during the moments when he wasn't covering his eyes.

But then a rental car pulled between them, clearly driven by someone from out of state, lost, flustered and clueless about how to remain alive behind the wheel in Los Angeles. It took mere moments for that driver to lose control of his vehicle and spin off the road and down a small embankment in front of one of the multi-million dollar homes.

"Enough!" shouted Wimp, and he reached for the wheel and turned it hard and although Butch glared, she managed to steer the car onto a side road and then down a ways out of the action. Then she stopped the car to catch her breath.

"That's it! It's over. We're going home, right now. Move it!" said Wimp forcefully.

Butch's jaw dropped and instinctively she reached for the crop beside her, but before she could grasp it, he had snatched it from her, easily snapping it in two across his thigh. He tossed it defiantly in the back seat and glared at her, his jaw rigid, his eyes steely.

Butch felt something inside her quiver a little, a new sensation, one she found enticingly erotic. "Oh, Glenn," she said, leaning in toward him.

He raised one eyebrow, extended his hand and pointed a finger in front of him. "Home I said. Now."

Kevin saw none of this although he was parked by the side of the road, observing the rental car buried deep in some expensive shrubbery. Did they have only one cop on Sunset Boulevard, that's what Kevin was wondering now, because true to his luck today, there was Officer Snotty Pants, and as a tow truck arrived to extricate the rental car and then, to Kevin's astonishment, to confiscate his Porsche, he shook his head. Clearly this day couldn't get any worse. That was when Billy the Kid handcuffed him and shoved him in the back seat of his cop car. Was everyone against him? Was there no justice, no rationality? Where was the serenity, that's what Kevin wanted to know. Where was the decency? Where was that fucking Honda?

In short order Kevin stood like a common criminal, being fingerprinted, and wiping his hands on his pants like some thug.

"It's digital, pal, no ink," said the station cop ruefully. "You know, doc, you coulda just paid the fines. All these outstanding tickets really worked against you. You're just lucky they didn't hold you overnight."

Kevin was aghast. "Pay fines? Like hell I will. I'm fighting this all the way. Supreme Court here I come. Someone is chasing me off the road and some infant who became a cop like yesterday gives me ticket after ticket—I don't think so."

The cop shook his head. He'd seen it all, but never before had anyone involved in a car crash played the Supreme Court card. At least the guy wasn't drunk although he did smell strongly of chocolate, and what was that other smell? Gummy bears? Maybe it was some sugar rush induced manic incident. It could happen, he supposed. "Okay, fine. Here's what you need. Court date on Monday. Eventually they'll release the car to you, after all this is settled."

Kevin accepted some documents from the cop and said, "What?"

"Assault with a deadly weapon—your car—it's a serious charge."

"That little pissant," said Kevin. "Can I go now?"

"Do you need me to call you a cab?"

Laura had refused Bill's offer to stay at his place for the night and insisted she'd be fine at home, precisely where she wanted to be, so he watched her drive away and sat for a moment outside his house to talk to the kids. He didn't want them to be shocked when they got inside, or sad about what had happened.

"I guess you noticed Chrissy wasn't at the party even though it was supposed to be for her," he started calmly. His voice was balanced and he hoped he could keep it that way so the kids would feel safe and not get upset. They had to be told and he had to remain steady for them. Both kids shrugged as he continued, "Chrissy won't be there when we get inside. She's not going to live with us any more. I guess you'd say we broke up. Sometimes these things happen with grown-ups. I just want you to know how sorry I am about everything. Nothing's more important to me than the two of you, and I really hope you know that. Yes things will change, but I'll still be here and you can count on me to take care of you, not just today but always. And we're still a family, you know that, right? No matter what, we'll always be a family."

"Thank God," said Will, "I was worried you might marry her. I could picture you dead and me pushing her in a wheel chair toward some old folks' diet center." He shuddered.

"So you're not upset it's just us again?" Bill asked surprised, although on some level he knew he shouldn't feel that way.

"Hey Dad she's nuts."

"Jessica says it was a midnight crisis," added Candy.

"Why didn't you tell me all this sooner? I mean I knew you had misgivings but not to this extent."

"Jessica was afraid to shock you in such a delicate condition," Candy said seriously.

"Jessica is certainly a very deep young lady," said Bill, smiling. "And how does she have all this life wisdom, I wonder."

"Oh her mom's boyfriend's some kind of doctor. Wait, wait, I know what it is." Candy squinted and wiggled her hands, trying to bring up the word she couldn't remember.

"That guy her mom's dating's a doctor? That young guy who calls everyone dude? No, I don't think so," said Will. "He's barely older than me."

Bill looked up in shock at what he was hearing. Jessica's mom had some boy toy in what, high school? No, that couldn't be true. "What?" he said lamely.

"Mixology!" Candy exclaimed, "Doctor of Mixology, that's what Jessica said. That's the doctor who fixes people who're all mixed up."

"How did you ever make it through Kindergarten?" asked Will.

"What do you mean," said Candy, "I can color inside all the lines, you know I can."

The kids seemed all right, Bill thought, relieved, as they opened the car doors and walked toward the house. He'd screwed up royally, but they seemed okay. He'd let a woman move into their mother's home and he pretended she belonged there when he should have been paying more attention. He should have shown better paternal instincts. He had been selfish and hasty and Bill felt ashamed. He'd done a very poor job indeed with everything. But the kids seemed all right. They seemed smarter than he did. At least he had that.

Tomorrow he would hire a housekeeper. The maid who came several times a week wasn't enough. He'd find some nice, motherly woman to be there after school and life would seem normal even if it wasn't. Well it would seem better. And they would begin again and would all have each other. It would all work out. He didn't really know if it would work out, but each time he said that to himself he felt better, so every day he would say it and one day it would be true. Together they would start another brave new chapter, the last thing on earth Bill wanted, but as he had no choice, this time he would do it better and maybe he would get it right.

NINE

If Kevin had been a cartoon, the steam would have been visibly rising from the top of his head. As it was, he sighed, he seethed, and he dialed his cell phone. Kevin stood in front of the Beverly Hills police station, which really was quite splendid. They'd rebuilt it and the architecture and design were lovely — which in his current state of rage he considered a laughable waste of money. If there had been a suggestion box handy, Kevin would have informed them it made more sense just to use an insane asylum if everyone who worked there was going to be a deranged idiot and then taxpayer's money could be spent funding donut shops, which would make everyone happy except his patients.

Laura was indulging in some self-medicating, her guilty pleasure — a cup of hot chocolate with whipped cream on top. The puppy was in her lap as she sat on the couch, her legs tucked up under her, a soft and comforting robe wrapped around her. Now and then she'd give the puppy a little lick of whipped cream on her finger.

When the phone rang, she answered it without thinking, not even bothering to look at the caller I.D. "Hello?"

"Thank God you're home," said Kevin, sounding particularly harried.

Laura didn't bother to wonder why. Chances are he hadn't screwed any other women tonight and if he were being held up at gunpoint he probably wouldn't be allowed to make a call. If he'd been kidnapped, well she'd read *The Ransom of Red Chief* long ago in school and she knew who'd get the worst of that deal.

Kevin shook his phone. They'd been disconnected. What in blazes? Was this sinkhole of a police station a dead zone for cell signals as well as brain waves? He pressed the button again and the phone began to ring. And ring. And ring. Soon he heard the sound of his own voice, something that normally he would find appealing but tonight to listen to himself saying *you've reached the home of Doctor Kevin Flicker. Please leave a message...* was far too much to bear after all the humiliation he'd endured.

Kevin began walking, but it was quite dark and he assumed all the police were off arresting nuns or throwing parades for drunk drivers, so he reached into his wallet, wondering if he had a card for a limo service. Why not treat himself? He deserved it after being practically raped by a chocoholic and subjected to who knew how many germs in the police asylum. But the only card he found was that girl's, that caterer girl, what'sername, here it was right here, Angie. He guessed he could show them. Bill always telling him to back off. Laura always treating him like a leper. Here was someone, a nice little someone, and she was hot. And hot for him. But did she have a car? Who knew. Well, he was about to find out.

And find out he did. Once he was seated in the passenger seat being driven along by this sweet little cupcake, Kevin finally started to calm down—he refused to give in to the paranoia and looked out the window only intermittently. His voice sounded calm, he was pretty sure it did.

"Of course you're not going to a hotel," Angie said, "I have plenty of room."

"What a night," said Kevin. Look at that. She was patting his hand. What a little sweetheart. Kevin grasped her hand and held it tightly, feeling the strains of the worst day ever melt away. And as long as he didn't think too much, he almost felt good.

At least they weren't on Sunset. That phrase echoed through Kevin's mind now and then and each time it did, he squeezed Angie's hand. She'd driven through the shopping area of Beverly Hills and had turned south of Wilshire. It didn't take long. And they didn't take Sunset.

At the same moment Angie's dad was returning home from a political fund raiser. He'd treated himself to a brand new car and was proud he hadn't fallen into the Mercedes trap of virtually all his colleagues. He wanted something simple. A small SUV was the way to drive, not too much gas, nobody to impress.

"Oh my God," shrieked Kevin, his voice at about the octave range usually reserved for pre-pubescent boys or those deliberately sheared of their genitalia in order to maintain those high notes. "Quick, turn around. Go around the block." Frantically he reached for the wheel, but Angie shrugged, asked no questions, and just did as he asked.

Angie's dad had driven into his garage and lowered the door. Should he have gotten red or a jazzier color? Of course not. He wasn't having a mid-life crisis. He'd just bought a car. A nice, neat little black Honda CR-V. Like a Jeep but better. Fantastic ratings and resale value. A sane person's car. And you could easily put your dog in the back. If you had a dog. Maybe he would get a dog — Angie had said she wanted one.

It took about two minutes for Angie and Kevin to circle the block and all the while Kevin's head spun frantically around, looking in vain for the Honda. "We outwitted them," he said jovially, "They're gone," and then instantly terrified, "Do you really think they're gone?"

"Who?"

Kevin attempted to appear sociable and even nonchalant as they entered the guesthouse when what he wanted to do was dim all the lights and stand guard at the window. It took full concentration for him to speak casually, to look around socially and comment on his surroundings, "Nice place. And you rent this guest house? I might be in the market for something like it soon." Self control could be maintained only so long, as Kevin knew only too well, and so he skulked to the window and standing covertly to the side, peered out.

"It's my dad's. He has the main house."

"Well it's got everything you need, doesn't it." There was a kitchen on one wall at the rear, a big brass bed on another and a little sitting area with a love seat and a television. Maybe he could fix up the guest house at his place like this in case Laura insisted he leave for a few days.

"I'm going to change," whispered Angie.

"Oh don't change," said Kevin absently, "You're so nice the way you are."

"I meant my clothes."

Kevin barely noticed as she walked down a small hallway into a dressing room, giving him a chance to focus his full energy on what potentially lurked outside the window. A car drove down the street and he jumped, but he could see it wasn't *the* car. Just a car.

In a blur Kevin found himself naked, in bed, being kissed and touched by a girl who had hands, hands that could knead bread. But what? He was thinking about bread? And he couldn't see out the window, but he could see lights passing now and then and he jumped each time a car passed. He knew he had to get a grip. They surely would not mow through the side walls of this guesthouse and run him down. Would they? They surely would not be waiting in the bushes to jump him when he walked out the door in the morning? Would they? Without his car around him, Kevin felt naked. And he actually was naked. With a sandwich girl. Come to think of it—he hadn't had anything to eat in hours. She opened a drawer and he wondered if there was a sandwich in there and then he was pretty sure his blood sugar had plummeted to some never before experienced low. Not a sandwich. A condom. And then something else plummeted. This was a day of firsts. Everything you never wanted to have happen and less. Or more. Or was it less?

He sat up in the bed, the covers pulled up to his chin for the second time in hours, and beside him the girl did the same. If he'd been this miserable before, he couldn't remember when. Wait? Was that a car? He shook his head, trying to regain his sanity.

"I should leave," he said.

"Don't be silly. You're just stressed." Angie sighed. "You *are* stressed, right? I mean, um, it's not cause, um, you remember how I looked before, it's not is it?"

"Oh, baby." Kevin hugged the sandwich girl and tried to sound rational. "It's hard to be, um hard, with assassins chasing you."

Angie shrugged. It happened. Well, she knew it happened. She'd heard it happened. "Let's just get some sleep."

"Perfect," said Kevin. "You've been a real sport tonight. I really do thank you. And tomorrow I will thank you properly. Or improperly." He thought about offering to order a pizza but somehow that just seemed rude. He had to maintain some level of decorum, didn't he? If you allow a girl to drag you to her apartment instead of checking into a hotel, you forfeit the right to call room service, don't you?

Angie smiled sweetly at him. It happened, so wasn't it better just to be understanding?

Kevin lay there all night, intermittently looking out the window and toward the fridge. By the morning he was doubly frazzled, exhausted, and starving. At least that's what he told himself when something that had never happened before happened again. Had that cop somehow put a curse on him? No, he didn't believe that. He hunkered down into the softness of the bed, pulling the covers over his head morosely, even when the nice girl tried to snuggle him. He had a curse on his head, so what good did that do. No, a curse on his dick. The worst curse of all. A wurst curse, he thought sardonically and then that he really needed to eat something.

"You must still be upset. It's okay, really it is."

"So it's come to this. Torture and humiliation. I've gotta get out of here."

"I'll drive you."

It took just moments for Angie and Kevin to be ready to leave, but in those very same moments, Angie's dad had pulled out of his garage and began backing down the driveway. Seeing the car, Kevin leapt into the air, and in a particularly intense display of the fight or flight phenomenon, he dashed forward and began banging on the car in a rage, causing Antimangia to stop and exit the vehicle. Expecting the respect and reticence he was always granted, he was astonished when Kevin grabbed him by the lapel and started screaming.

"Who the fuck are you and what the fuck do you think you're doing?" Kevin held Antimangia in a tight grip, and shook him repeatedly. "Answer me, dammit."

"Let go of me, you lunatic."

Angie ran up to Kevin and pushed against him but his adrenalin rush was too strong. She shouted, "Stop it Kevin, he's my dad. Stop it. Stop it. He's my dad."

Kevin snorted with disbelief. Was she in on it? It wasn't a dick curse, it was a conspiracy. "He's an assassin. Who's behind this? My wife? Come clean, right now or this is going to get ugly."

Angie grew frantic, pushing against Kevin to no effect. Being fat would have come in handy now, but she wasn't heavy enough to knock a man his size off balance and her dad, smaller than Kevin, might end up crushed on the ground. Luckily Ben drove up and dashed out of his car and ran up, grabbed the hose and doused Kevin with it, who registered shock, then let go of Angie's dad long enough for him to step back out of reach.

Ben stared at everyone. He spotted Kevin, the quack. And he looked at Angie who seemed to be both guilty when looking at him and triumphant when gazing toward her dad.

"Angie, call the cops," said her dad.

Her voice sounded worried but inside Angie secretly felt a little thrilled. But why? Were they fighting over her? It didn't seem like that. "Everyone calm down. It's just a mistake."

Chrissy was thankful for two things. First of all, her membership at the gym was paid up for many months to come. Secondly, she still had one of Bill's credit cards and the money she'd saved during the year she'd lived with him — it was at least a thousand dollars and that was a pretty good chunk of change. She wondered what the rents were now and remembered how difficult it had been to make the rent before he'd come along. Roommates, she'd had three. Chrissy shuddered. But she knew it might come to her knocking on their door — if any of them still lived there — and begging to stay on the couch for a while. What a horrific possibility. She'd managed to pack most of her clothing and personal items into the trunk of her old VW bug, a car she hadn't driven in the year she'd been with Bill, preferring instead to drive his wife's little Mercedes convertible. She wondered if she could get that car in the divorce. He'd been unfaithful. If only she had proof. And if only they were actually married.

Her stress level was monumental and she couldn't think clearly. No matter how many additional diet pills she swallowed, she didn't feel in charge. In fact she felt decidedly out of whack. Her inner hum was off. Her heart felt different. Was this a broken heart? Chrissy didn't know. The thing she had feared most had happened but although stressed, she didn't feel that sad. Did she miss Bill and the vipers? Not really. Did she miss her at-home gym and walk-in closet? Most definitely.

The real question was what was her next move. What did she want, and the one thing she wanted unquestionably was to be thin, to be as thin as she knew she should, could, and deserved to be. And there was only one way to do that. But how. How could she go to India to seek the one aid that would guarantee her permanent thinness? She didn't speak Indian and what if nobody there spoke English? How would she make herself clear? She needed some sort of group tour, perhaps one she could organize of people like herself who needed that drug and weren't willing to wait for the American health machine to grind forward. But how?

Pondering these weighty issues, she thundered along on the treadmill at a swift pace when Butch and Wimp entered Zero Tolerance. There was something different about them and it took a moment for Chrissy to discern what it was—their usual leather garb was gone. They were wearing normal street attire—Butch was even in a dress. Wow, she looked very non-butch. They seemed to spot her, glance toward each other nervously and try subtly to move in another direction. Was Chrissy crazy? But she waved and of course they came over to say hello, so perhaps her mind was playing tricks on her. It had happened before.

Chrissy told them the whole sad story about Bill kicking her out—completely without provocation on the eve of that stupid smoking fund raiser, though why Bill and Laura were so determined to fund the tobacco companies Chrissy had no idea—weren't they very rich businesses? Who knew what wealthy people dabbled in, not her but she wished she were still in a position to dabble.

Butch and Wimp looked properly aghast but somehow a bit distant from the whole story when before they were always so invested. Why was that, Chrissy wondered.

"And all my gym equipment is still there at his place and of course I have nowhere to take it. No idea about how to handle that."

"Maybe you could sell it," said Wimp, unusually assertive Chrissy thought, and she waited for the crop to come down on him, but for some reason Butch had forgotten it. It was frustrating that you could never count on people to be as you'd come to expect them to behave. "I know a guy," Wimp said, reaching into his gym bag and writing down an address on a piece of paper. "Maybe you could swing by there and discuss it with him after your workout here. Sorry I don't have the number."

"Well, thanks so much," said Chrissy, thinking she'd rather blow her brains out than lose her gym, but at least she had this place. "I'm just sort of worried about going back to Bill's—he seemed pretty enraged last time we were together. I'm a little afraid and wish I had someone to come along with me."

"We gotta run," said Butch improbably, and off they went, not even stopping to work out. Who does that, thought Chrissy, come to the gym and not work out. Were they just coming to see her?

It was like one of those aha moments. Chrissy decided why sell her equipment. She could rent a storage unit, so after the workout she drove toward a place that she'd often passed and went inside. It was perfect. There was even electricity inside some of the units and that way if she needed to plug in, she could. Handing Bill's credit card to the guy, she said, "I'll take it for a year." Then she watched as he ran the card four times until he looked at her and said, "Sorry, Miss, this card has been cancelled."

That rat! That skunk! That Malomar eating, cheating cheapskate. No wonder she'd cheated on him, no wait, he'd cheated on her. Who was that palimony lawyer? If only she could remember the name. For now though Chrissy knew what she had to do and glumly she drove toward the address Wimp had given her. She pulled into the parking lot and walked inside, quickly making an arrangement to sell her equipment in a few hours to a congenial guy. It had been easy and since the guy would be meeting her at Bill's, she would be safe.

Chrissy walked back to her car, knowing she couldn't remain at the hotel. Even though they'd run Bill's card successfully when she checked in, surely they would reject it when it was time to leave. As Chrissy didn't want to waste her little bit of money on a pricey hotel, she was about to dial the number of her old roommate when her attention was drawn to something next door.

Hypnotic music played softly and there were people entering in brightly colored robes. They looked so happy and serene. In front of the building was an easel holding a framed poster proclaiming, *Meet Guru Majee Today.* And there in the picture was a knowing Indian woman with one of those dots on her forehead. How interesting. Chrissy looked at the sign above door and it said *Temple of the Slender Thread.* How phenomenal, she thought, and in the door she went.

Ben and Clint walked along the sidewalk toward Angie's deli, Colette between them for what was supposed to be a get acquainted lunch. "Gosh I hope you and Angie like each other," said Ben to Colette, who had instantly become one of his best friends.

"No, no, no," she said rather adorably, "That would be a huge mistake. Huge. She has to hate me. I'm the enemy."

"I know. I get it. I understand your plan, but I'm just not sure it makes any sense. It just seems too duplicitous."

"Dude," said Clint, "This is shock therapy. Colette is right. Sometimes girls have to see a guy with another girl, realize they could lose him."

"But does it really make sense to trick her into falling for me? Not like she hasn't had plenty of time to do it on her own."

Colette put her hand gently on Ben's arm. "We're not tricking her. We're helping her snap out of her psychosis and wake up to the reality she really wants but doesn't know it, the guy she was meant to be with but never realized. It's not a trick, it's a kick in the pants."

Ben smiled at Colette then looked toward Clint. It was rather odd that he was tagging along, wasn't it? Maybe their other plan was working too. "What if I act like I'm head over heels for you then Clint steals you away from me? Then Angie would feel sorry for me. Maybe that's a better script."

"Dude! Do you really want to be the runt puppy that nobody wants except some old lady with one bad eye?" Clint scowled at Ben as though he were pathetic. "For a smart guy it's like you're too clueless to be real."

"Forget about scripts," said Colette. "Just go with it. Just react to what I do."

"And I'm just there cause we're friends. I'm not some girl stealer. What kind of a rat do you think I am?" asked Clint.

"Okay, okay," said Ben. "Once more unto the breach...imitate the action of the tiger."

Clint looked perplexed for a moment then seemed to relate and said, "Exactly, dude, eye of the tiger."

"Men!" said Colette, hoisting her heavy tote from Clint's arm and onto her shoulder as they entered the deli, which was quite full with a happily dining lunchtime crowd. There was just one empty table, designed for only two, which Colette pointed toward as Angie emerged from the kitchen to greet them.

Ben examined her carefully. Had the embarrassment of the morning registered on her? She seemed rather subdued and he wondered did she wish they didn't already have these plans.

"Hey guys," said Angie, seemingly nonchalantly, "And you must be Colette, nice to meet you." She smiled and even hugged Colette who hugged her back.

"Mmm," said Colette particularly sweetly, "Bacon! You smell like bacon. Yum!"

Angie squinted and scowled a bit then said, "I wasn't cooking bacon."

"You mean it's your natural scent?" asked Colette sweetly, "How piggylicious. No wonder my honey loves you."

Angie was aghast. People thought she smelled like bacon? This was supposed to be a compliment? Who was this girl, anyway, and what was Ben doing with her? "If you just wait a couple minutes I'll be able to give you a bigger table and we'll all sit," she said a bit frostily.

"Don't be silly," said Colette, "My honey pie is hungry, aren't you honey pie?" She looked toward Ben and tickled him under the chin. Then she pushed him toward one of the two empty chairs, dumped her bag on the ground and lowered herself into his lap, wrapping her arms around his neck. "Could I do this at a bigger table?" Then she laughed lustily and said, "You betcha. Oh don't you just love this man! Think of the babies we're gonna make. Maybe tonight!" As Ben's eyes opened wide with astonishment, Colette put her hand on his face and turned it away from Angie and toward her and kissed him tightly on the mouth several times. "Better than lunch!" she said.

Clint looked up at the ceiling, down at the floor, then decided he could pull off suave and said, "You two crazy kids."

Ben didn't know where to look. He glanced furtively at Angie to see if she was reacting in any way at all, and she did seem to have a disapproving look on her face, so maybe that was something. Maybe one day they'd laugh together about this.

A larger table had opened up and Angie pointed toward it saying, "It'll be a lot easier for us to eat if we all have seats."

"If you insist," said Colette, "But wait, I need a little amuse bouche before I give up the best seat in the house." And once more she began kissing Ben. After several kisses on the lips, she began kissing his neck with rather loud slurping sounds and much noise, then she laughed and said, "They don't call them smackeroos for nothing."

Once they were all seated, Angie returned from the kitchen with some sampler plates of her latest menu items and some tasting plates. "No more cutting edge cuisine," she said to Ben.

"Oh my honey pie likes down home good cooking, don't you sugar lump? We're gonna bring back the old times, that's for sure, once we move into our house. And it will be so much fun driving cross country together until we get back home."

"What?" said Clint and Angie simultaneously.

"Well we're just not city folk, are we honey pie? We're thinking Iowa or Ohio, one of the really good states with the short names."

"Really?" Angie asked Ben.

"Now, now, Angie-dangie, don't you go confusing my honey pie. You had him all to yourself since you were toddlers, but now it's my turn. We have to have a nice big yard for all those babies to run around in, don't we?" Colette reached into her tote and pulled out several magazines. "Check this out—look at this darling house—what a little love nest." She took Ben's hand and pressed it fervently to her chest and said, "Oh honey pie, feel my heart beating. Just for you!" Then she took a forkful of food off her plate and leaned in toward Ben and said, "Open wide. Here comes the airplane." Then she laughed as Ben obeyed and said, "Just practicing for when Ben junior comes."

"Maybe you'll have twins," said Clint good naturedly. "Ben junior and Ben junior-junior."

"Mmm, yum-o," said Colette to Angie, "This tuna salad is fabuloso, almost as good as my mom's."

"It's duck," said Angie.

"Rubber ducky, you're the one," sang Colette, running her hand through Ben's hair in a mock shampoo. "Oh my God!" she trilled, displaying an enormous amount of excitement, and waving her hands in the air a few times, said "I totally forgot," then reached back down into her tote and extracted an elegant parcel from which she pulled a white lace nightgown. "Look at this, Angie, wait, Ben, cover your eyes, no what the heck, might as well have a little preview. Oh, can you imagine me in this?" And then she stood and held the lingerie up to herself, turning this way and that with many seductive wriggles.

Ben blushed and Colette laughed, "Oh isn't he just too good to be true. What a dirty mind. He's picturing me out of it, aren't you honey pie?"

Bill sighed as he walked out of his attorney's office and back to his own where he would have the girls go through all the patient files and see who belonged to whom. This was going to be as bad as a divorce. There would be patients to placate, assets to split up, decisions about locations. It was a huge headache. He couldn't legally bar Kevin from the office. Being a sleaze ball didn't disqualify him from practicing medicine. He would have to confront Kevin, perhaps more than once and attorneys might have to be present. Papers would have to be drawn up. Even if he found a new office, which he probably would have to do, there would still be much contact. But did it matter that much? He was angry at Kevin, yes. He didn't want to associate with Kevin any longer, no. But did he feel that the sight of Kevin would send him into a rage? Bill didn't know. Despite the fact that he clearly was better off without Chrissy, he knew that having a partner who'd do such a thing was out of the question. Kevin's ethics had always been a problem but the truth was that he'd never treated Kevin as a partner, more of a junior associate, and certainly Kevin resented that. Should Bill be assuming some of the blame for this situation? Surely that would be absurd. He would just have to deal with the aggravations until he was extricated. And then life would go on and he probably would never see Kevin again.

He could ask Laura to help him find a new office. Laura would know a real estate person. It seemed such a strange thought—now that there was no party to plan, he and Laura surely wouldn't be spending as much time together. And he recognized that she had been correct—for them to end up together would be sort of tacky. His partner screwed his girlfriend so Bill should snag Kevin's wife? Was it wrong? It probably was. What was it he had been feeling for Laura anyway? Had she been right? Was he just using her as some sort of conduit to the past? Were they playing musical chairs and were they the only two people left in the game so it seemed reasonable for them to end up together? Having a good old friend by his side would be nice, it would be lovely, wouldn't it? Bill admitted that it would. But somewhere deep inside his heart he admitted something else. Laura had been right—that was no substitute for love. And then Bill admitted the thing that was most heart wrenching, the thing he didn't want to think let alone say out loud. He had no faith that he would be thunderstruck by love ever again. That sort of intense connection didn't just happen because JoEllen was a one in a million and it wasn't as though there were more just like her standing on every corner, were there. And then his heart sank.

Was he destined always to be alone? His sudden lurch toward Laura, if it had been what she'd assumed, some sort of desperate attempt to settle for next best, was as pathetic as she'd presumed. And so was he. Perhaps he would have to come to grips with the idea that this part of his life was over. And it was just so terribly sad. For it wasn't just the idea of not being with the love of his life that he missed, it was the togetherness, the family activities, the couple activities, the companionship. If the one and only love of his life was dead, did that mean all the casual stuff that accompanied a great love affair was beyond his reach as well?

He did have the kids of course, and they would always be a family, so he didn't lose that. But somehow it had seemed that being with the wrong woman was better than being with no woman. So those were his choices — being a dad but not a husband or inflicting the wrong woman on his children so he could have some tepid adult companionship? It all seemed so bleak. His prior resolve to remind himself that everything would all work out seemed to have dissolved and he was back in the abyss of loneliness, emptiness, and misery.

It was quite tempting to allow himself to sink down into that depressed state of mind, but Bill had been there far too long and he chose instead to get a grip. Perhaps his days with the perfect mate — or any mate — were over but he could find some happiness, he would have to try to find happiness, to do things that he'd enjoy, in groups or even alone, when he wasn't spending time with the kids. He could take the sort of advice he always gave lonely patients — do something, take a class, find a hobby, reach out to casual acquaintances and turn them into friends, throw a party. Well, maybe not that last one.

Bill lumbered through his day, concealing the emotional issues that weighed on him from his patients — and Kevin's patients — for Kevin hadn't shown up and the confrontation had thus not taken place — and he managed to smile, to do his job, and to take care of everyone. He'd engaged a housekeeper perhaps too quickly, but she came well recommended and thus someone was there with the kids after school. He was getting a grip, at last he was doing that.

He dialed Laura's number. At the least he owed her an apology.

"Hey there, Bill," she said without any preliminary hello. Apparently she was now checking her caller ID.

"How are you?" he said. "Doing okay?"

"Sure, I'm okay. You?"

"Coping. I'm really calling mainly to apologize. I'm so sorry for my behavior the other night. I know it was tacky. I hope you can forgive me."

"It's okay. I know you're stressed and desperate."

"Gee, stressed and desperate. If only I were doing a resume. Or a personal ad." Bill laughed.

Laura laughed too. "Well you know what I mean."

"Did you make up with Kevin? He hasn't been in to work. In fact I saw a lawyer today. When they say breaking up is hard to do they mean it literally."

"So at least one of us is divorcing him," said Laura a little ruefully.

"You mean only one of us is?"

"All I've done so far is hang up on him. For all I know he's in Haiti divorcing me."

"So would that be a bad thing?"

"Probably not."

"I'm really sorry. I feel responsible somehow."

"Why—did you screw him too?"

Bill laughed. "He probably thinks I did. Or that I will. Looks like if I want my divorce I'll have to move because I can't really make him move. Of course I haven't seen him to discuss it."

"Give it some time," said Laura reasonably.

"So you're saying just take him back, don't end the partnership? I can't do that. It'll be a pain in the neck but it has to be done. And I might need your help—real estate—need to find a new office. I'm sorry to be asking forgiveness and another favor simultaneously."

"Yeah," said Laura, "How dare you!" Then she laughed and gave him the name of a real estate person.

"Thanks, hon. You're always prepared. I love that about you."

"Yup, once a Girl Scout…."

Laura sounded truly miserable Bill thought. "I wish I could do something to cheer you up," he said. "Would you want to have dinner, with the kids maybe? I could cook or we could go out."

"Oh I dunno. I'm not exactly hungry."

"Is there anything I can do then?"

"Suggest a good vet for neutering maybe?"

"For the puppy? Is it that time already?"

"No, for Kevin."

TEN

Kevin had faith in the justice system. They didn't make twerps judges, of course they didn't. During this entire nightmare he had been dealing with the wrong people, well in fact a single individual, that idiot boy in blue. Now he would have his day in court and he could envision himself explaining rationally the horrific situation to a kindly elder jurist, someone with experience, wisdom, and intelligence. Then it would all be over, except for the warrant for the arrest for that rogue driver, which Kevin did realize would be difficult to fulfill because he didn't have so much as a digit from the license plate or a description. But those were just the details, weren't they, not the actual fact.

The fact was that Kevin was a respected doctor and that meant something in Beverly Hills. And when he spoke, people listened. Today it would be a judge listening to him and this mess would be on its way to a solution. Then Kevin could get on with his life. Everything would be resolved and hopefully that maniac would ultimately be in jail.

Kevin pondered the situation. There was that supposed father of the seemingly nice sandwich girl. It was tempting to consider it a conspiracy, but he had been treating this girl for many months and pulling off a caper like that would be virtually impossible. Come in fat, get thin, months later her pseudo (or real) father begins attempting to run him off the road. Even at his most irrational he couldn't concede the probability of this conjecture—and Kevin had eaten regularly in the last couple of days and knew that his low blood sugar had been resolved, thus extinguishing any metabolic lack of clarity. More likely was it that in this instance Cop Crapper was correct—it was a popular car, the man was the girl's father, and by coincidence the vehicles were the same.

Kevin thought briefly about the other driver. Who that was he had no idea. No matter to what extent Laura was angry at him, she would not instigate anything as insane as this ongoing road rage. It just wasn't like her. And nobody else was angry at him, were they? Bill was angry just now but there was no way a guy as rigid and dull as Bill would pull such a stunt and besides, Bill was clearly shocked to find him in bed with the chocolate queen, and the chases had been going on before this occurred, so clearly it wasn't Bill. That left—nobody. What a puzzle.

And then Kevin realized something at once comforting and distressing—it was a case of mistaken identity. Perhaps it was the car. Maybe someone else, someone in the line of fire, drove a car like his and they were following him by mistake. Maybe they even had the number from his license plates, surely they did. That meant that it would be extremely difficult to find them because no connection existed between Kevin and them. It was like Strangers on a Train or one of those other thrillers from another era. There was only one solution. Kevin would have to sell his car.

Oh how this realization triggered pangs in his heart. He had loved that Porsche from the moment he'd bought it and even more since this psychosis had been visited upon him because of the security it provided him by being the excellent vehicle it was. He didn't really see himself in a Ferrari—and that was buckets of dough, plastic surgeon dough, anesthesiologist dough, not internist dough. So where did it leave him? He'd have to consider his options. This was a true tragedy and utterly unfair.

Briefly Kevin thought about what was imminently to come and the fact that he hadn't even engaged a lawyer. He had called the attorney who drew up the papers for the practice and was informed that he could not be represented because Bill had a prior claim. More psychosis he would have to unravel. Perhaps the partnership would end. Nobody looking over his shoulder and complaining about every little thing. How could he tolerate that? No, he'd be fine without Bill and today without a lawyer. He was intelligent, articulate, for Christ's sake, he was a doctor.

Standing erect, his clothes expensive and well pressed, Kevin strode into the courtroom and took a seat. Soon he would have his justice. Thank the lord. Look—there was Billy the Kid sitting off in the distance. He hoped to mop up the floor with that moron.

Then the bailiff entered and spoke. "All rise, court of Honorable Justice Samuel A. Antimangia presiding."

That was a familiar sounding name, Kevin thought. Where had he heard that name before? He couldn't quite place it. And then Angie's dad entered the court in his robes and locked eyes with Kevin, both men glaring like bulls who'd just been engaged by a matador.

Naturally he called Kevin's case first.

Kevin took a deep breath, remained calm and said confidently, "Your honor I am an innocent party here. Someone has been trying to run me off the road."

"I've heard," said the judge snidely.

"It's clearly a case of mistaken identity. I've finally determined that. Nobody in my life would be responsible for this constant vehicular harassment."

"Why sell yourself short," said the judge jauntily, squinting toward Kevin with wrath in his eyes. "They'd probably fight for the privilege."

"I've been victimized and traumatized several times, all without the help I deserved."

"No psychiatrists on your speed dial?" asked the judge sardonically, as Kevin look horrified at this rancid little man. "I've heard enough," said Antimangia preemptively.

"But your honor...."

"You realize I could put you in jail?" asked the judge, while Kevin nodded miserably and remained silent. The bailiff looked quizzically at the judge, someone he knew to behave as a cranky old sod, despite not being as old as he acted, as Antimangia, who was a decent judge, rambled, "I'd love to put you in jail, no not jail, prison. Death row."

The bailiff cocked his head toward the judge and the stenographer looked up, not wanting what she was hearing to go on the record, but the judge was invested in his comments and neither of them could interrupt.

"Capital punishment is underrated, I think." As Antimangia said this, the people in the courtroom seats registered a visible level of nervousness. If it were the old West, they'd be whispering that he was a hangin' judge.

"What happened to those chain gangs?" posited the judge. "Liberals, that's what happened to them. Frizzy headed women lawyers, that's what happened to them. Humanitarian — if you ask me, it's a four letter word."

Far in the back, a young man wearing shirt sleeves and shorts — the vacation clothes he'd brought on the trip, never expecting to need dressier attire in casual Los Angeles, leaned in close to an attorney next to him and whispered, "Just plead me guilty."

The lawyer put a steadying hand on the man's arm and replied, "You're the guy he ran off the road."

The bailiff leaned over to speak to the judge, words nobody heard, then Antimangia passed sentence. "Fine of $2,000, damages to cover auto repair and $5,000 emotional injury for that young fellow over there, six months community service, psychiatric evaluation. Must be some clinic somewhere that needs a free quac — doctor. And stay the hell away from my...courtroom.... And anywhere else I happen to be. Do you get me?"

Kevin nodded. Some justice, he thought, but he was too terrified to speak up.

Bill observed Chrissy parking on the street by his house, but he noted that she didn't exit her car. He assumed she was waiting for the guys who were coming to pick up her exercise equipment. Technically that stuff belonged to Bill, who had paid for it, but it was bought for her and the last thing he wanted now was to be petty. What he did want to do was to examine his own heart and see what lurked inside. Would seeing Chrissy provoke any latent feelings for her or perhaps an insight or two? That was what Bill wondered. The kids were thankfully off on play dates so he didn't have to worry that they would suffer any further trauma. As far as they were concerned, Chrissy no longer existed and that would be true for him as well after the next few minutes.

Soon enough a truck parked in his driveway and a couple of guys walked toward the door with Chrissy. Somehow Bill didn't even feel enraged, just as though a business transaction were ending, as if he were selling an old car that was being removed. Oddly enough, it was Chrissy whose eyes shot daggers and Bill observed the withering glance she tossed him as she walked past him and into the den, her lackeys following her.

Chrissy was surprised when Bill had the gall to say hello to her considering how he'd behaved. Some people had such nerve, she thought, but not wanting to jeopardize the sale of her equipment, she smiled politely and said hello back, then walked right past him with the scorn he deserved.

The men got the machines out the door with a minor degree of aggravation as Bill and Chrissy stood silently together. "You've found a place already?" Bill asked kindly.

"I've found what I've always wanted, always needed," she said confidently.

Bill hoped she hadn't meant Kevin, for he knew that would be a huge mistake. Kevin never dallied and returned. "That sounds positive," he said neutrally.

"God knows you refused to get it for me," she said softly.

"Oh?"

"Don't pretend you don't know."

"What don't I know?"

"You do know. Koush Koush." Chrissy scowled at Bill.

"Really? Still?"

"You were just too busy porking your partner's porky wife to take my needs seriously," she said.

Bill was tempted to shove her out the door and lock it but shouldn't she know the actual truth? "We were never messing around. We were planning your birthday party."

"Yeah, right. At some smokers' rally. I wasn't born yesterday. I saw you two always lurking around together, shoving food into your mouths. Why don't you just be honest for once."

Bill laughed. "Honestly? I can't fathom how I spent a year with you."

Chrissy huffed and turned and followed the men out the door, accepted some cash from them and, without looking back, walked to her car and drove away as Bill made a mental note—if you hook up with women just because they casually resemble your dead wife, you get what you deserve.

Kevin was thinking about Meryl Streep and the fact that she had it much easier than he did. In *Sophie's Choice* she had two alternatives while he was being forced to sacrifice the thing he loved best, his beloved Porsche. There was no rational way he could allow himself to keep it. With demented, half-blind junior coppers and power-mad, moldy old judges ready to send him to the slammer for being an innocent victim, Kevin had to take self-protective measures. The car had to go. But what to do? Should he go and buy a BMW? A Corvette was sporty but had a different vibe than his Porsche. What a dilemma and a damn shame too.

He drove to the beach, all the way down on Pico Boulevard, where he had never seen that Honda and it had never pursued him. Hey, if Laura kicked him out permanently, maybe he could move down here and keep the car. No that was just silly. Laura would never kick him out permanently. They'd been married far too long. She would take him back and then punish him with her disgust and life would go on.

Just as he approached the ocean, Kevin had an inspiration. He had to sell the car, yes. He needed different license plates and a different color — but he could still have a Porsche. They weren't out there running down every freaking Porsche in the city, were they? He didn't actually know, but it was just obvious, wasn't it, that they were focused on him, or maybe on him and one or two others. He whipped the car onto Ocean Boulevard and then turned east onto Wilshire and soon enough he was back in Beverly Hills at the Porsche dealer, signing papers and driving away in a newer model, different plates, and a different color. Talk about the silver lining.

Then he decided it was time to confront Bill and get on with his career. Porsches didn't pay for themselves. He had a practice and he wasn't giving it up, so off he drove to the office, parking in his usual spot inside the building. He glanced at his watch — it was after six in the evening. Everyone was gone. But look — his name was still on the door, and his key still worked in the lock.

Kevin took a seat behind his desk. Really only a weekend and a day had passed, but it seemed as though he'd been gone forever. Perhaps it was the disjointed feeling of being away from home. He'd actually had to buy some new clothes, which as he thought of it was absurd. This was his office and that was his home. It wasn't as though he couldn't just walk in the door.

Laura was in the kitchen peeling carrots for dinner. It was a task that made her feel serene and she went about the work of cooking with a peaceful sense of pleasure. When the phone rang, she instinctively knew it was Kevin, and deciding that she couldn't ignore his calls forever, she answered the call.

"Honey!" he said fervently, "I know I have a lot to apologize for, and I'm sincerely sorry, but when you hear everything that's happened to me in the last few days I think you'll realize…" He paused to listen to what she was saying, then continued, "I know. I don't know what came over me…" More comments from Laura then he resumed speaking, "Yes it is some sort of malady. I don't know what, but once you hear my story about the car and that maniac."

Laura sighed. He was talking about the car, not the marriage. "I just don't know you any more."

"Let me come home. I promise to make it right. I'm never going to do anything like this again. I swear."

Laura lay down the peeler and thought for a moment. Her heart twisted inside her. She suspected that whatever choice she might make would be incorrect. "I don't know," she sighed, "I don't think I'm ready for that yet. Maybe not ever."

Kevin's voice grew irritated. "What else do you want from me? I said I'm sorry. What do you expect from me anyhow? You don't even know what I've gone through lately, what I've suffered. It's not like you even know I'm alive."

"Yes, Kevin, it was my fault you screwed your partner's bimbo. That and every other disgusting thing you've ever done. Clearly I should be begging your forgiveness instead of the other way around. Please forgive me for hanging up on your whoring ass." Laura slammed the phone back into its cradle and sat down on a stool at the counter, tears streaming down her cheeks.

Angie was feeling rather nervous as she parked her car in the driveway between the guesthouse and main residence. Gingerly removing a container, she walked softly to the side door and tapped on it. Her dad appeared rather too quickly, she thought, but she smiled brightly at him and tried to sound normal.

"Hi, Daddy! Here's some lasagna. Thought you might like a little snack."

The judge gestured dismissively at her, scowled his customary scowl, and growled crankily, "It's the middle of the night. Go to bed!"

Angie glanced at her watch. It wasn't even quite nine o'clock. She watched him gesture once again and then, without even taking the food from her hands, closed the door practically in her face. She stood there for a moment, just breathing, feeling hurt but also enraged.

"I hate it when you treat me like that. I'm angry at you," she said almost under her breath. "You're a lousy dad." Then even more softly, she whispered, "How was that, doctor?"

She turned to walk away, then turned back around and with one hand smashed the food down onto the doorstep, and with more than a little satisfaction watched it open and go splat all over the place. She should have done that long ago.

Kevin sat in the solitude of his office, his head in his hands. Despite the high of having a brand new car, he couldn't shake the feeling that in a few short days everything had turned to utter crap. Could it be possible that his life was in a downturn and might not recover? No, he didn't believe that. But what if it were true? What if life as he knew it were over? That could be true. A new car didn't make up for the security of losing his practice or his wife. How do you go from having everything, from life being wonderful, to being trapped in utter misery, that's what Kevin wanted to know. It was like some sort of bizarre Greek tragedy. Militant marauders come along and hustle you down some road toward chaos. How does that happen in real life?

Kevin took the little rake from his Zen garden and whacked the dangling balls on his Newton's Cradle, setting them aclatter. The noise was soothing, but it wasn't lost on Kevin that basically he was witnessing what he had recently endured — his equilibrium set out of balance by outside forces. Life was so strange.

What should he do to placate his wife, that was the main thing on Kevin's mind. Always in the past she was receptive to his promises and surely that meant something. Kevin wanted to believe it meant she loved him and trusted him and recognized that it was all just him letting off steam and didn't mean anything in the larger scheme of things. But could women really comprehend that? Shopping was what women did to let off steam but Laura had never been that big a shopper. She was a doer, she ran that anti-smoking thing, as though anyone who wanted to smoke could be persuaded to stop, but at least it was better than coming home daily with a cluster of shopping bags as did most doctors' wives. He was lucky. He had been lucky. The change of tense in his thoughts frightened Kevin. Perhaps it all was over.

Then his cell phone rang and Kevin grabbed it, pushing the button and prayerfully saying "Laura?"

"No, it's me, Angie." She stood at the back of her guesthouse in the tiny kitchen area, aggressively kneading a ball of dough on a flour-dusted cutting board. The rhythm of her movements was pleasant and calming and she could hear clearly through the speaker phone. Kevin sounded distraught again. What was up with him, she wondered. "Are you okay?"

He sighed heavily. "No. Your dad scared the shit out of me today."

Angie couldn't fathom that the morning's fracas could have been that traumatic for Kevin. "But you're twice his size and half his age. I thought for a bit you'd end up killing him."

Kevin laughed. It was nice to hear that he was big and young even though he knew that the judge was probably less than ten years his senior.

Angie was relieved to hear him chuckle. Maybe he wasn't as unhinged as he'd seemed previously. "Well we both know what he's like. How about coming over to finish what we started — well almost started."

"I can't run the risk of running into your dad. He'd have me shot."

"No sharpshooters tonight. He's in bed and asleep by ten. No way he'd spot you."

"I don't think so," said Kevin, sighing once more.

Angie's voice grew tremulous, and all the feelings for Kevin that for so long had been with her flooded over her, and the words poured out. "We were just so hot for each other before. And it's more than that, you know it is."

She really was sweet. And so uncomplicated. Kevin glanced at his watch. It wasn't that late. Where else did he have to go? "What the hell," he said.

Bill sat in the den with the kids, relaxing after a nice dinner out. Candy was on the floor with some papers, working hard on something for school, he assumed, because she was ignoring the movie that played on the TV, *Toy Story*, one of her favorites. Will, atypically, sat on the couch beside Bill, not attempting to torture his sister or create any disturbances. It was a pleasant family evening, something they really hadn't had in a very long time. Bill hadn't realized how Chrissy's absence would make such a difference. Everyone was calm and relaxed and it felt pretty good.

He couldn't resist asking Candy about her school project—maybe he could help. "What are you working on there, Miss Tootsie Pie?"

She looked up and said, "A very important list."

"Oh," said Bill, "Of what?"

"Well, Daddy, you might not know this, but I'm thinking it can work in our favor."

"What can?"

"The travesty of divorce."

Will laughed and said, "You mean the tragedy of divorce."

"Whatever," said Candy. "If I spent all my time thinking about the right word like you do, I'd never get anything said."

"There's a blessing we'll never see," said Will.

Candy stuck her tongue out at her brother, then resumed speaking to Bill. "Because of this travesty—um tragedy— whatever—there are a lot of single moms out there. Or non moms. Women, no husbands. That's where we come in."

"We do?" asked Bill, smiling.

"Look at you, Daddy. I mean take a look. Have you looked in the mirror lately?"

Bill thought about himself trying to squeeze into a too-small tuxedo only a few days ago. "I've looked," he said.

"So! I mean you're like Prince Charming, a total dreamboat, Mr. Right. So we just have to make the most of that."

Bill laughed and reached down and scooped Candy up in his arms and hugged her. "All little girls think their daddy is a dreamboat," he said, "It's the rules."

"C'mon, that's not true. Have you seen some of the daddies? I have. We're talking garbage barge, not dream boat."

Bill turned his head to one side and gazed at his daughter, who was so much like her mother. He smiled softly.

"So here's what I'm thinking," Candy said, jumping down from Bill's arms and grabbing her list from the floor. "We make a list of all the women who are possibles."

"We already had the impossible," said Will.

Candy nodded sagely, "Yes no more Miss Wrongs. We don't have forever and no point in wasting more time."

"So you're setting a deadline for me?" asked Bill. "Oh, the pressure!"

"I'm just saying why waste time. I can't go off to college with you here all alone. It wouldn't feel right."

"College?" asked Bill. "You're in second grade."

"Gramma says the older you get the faster time goes by. At your age it will probably feel like a week, maybe you have a month, I don't know. Do you really want to waste it joking around when you should be out there meeting a new wife?"

"Don't worry, Dad," said Will, smirking and pointing at his sister, "Nobody will ever marry Candy so that weirdo can be here taking care of you forever."

"How dare you," shrieked Candy. "I already have three boyfriends. I could marry any one of them I wanted to. I'm just taking my time."

"Lucky them," said Will.

"You...you...you..." sputtered Candy, "Thing Three! You're the worst Thing of all, greedy, selfish, monster."

Will laughed to see Candy so frustrated.

"Yeah well you're selfish, a total pig. But I'm a girl and there are things girls need to know that only a mom can tell them."

"What things?" asked Will.

"I don't know! There's no mom around here to tell me," shouted Candy, "That's why this is such a big emergency. You Thing!"

Bill looked at his frustrated daughter and reached out and took her hand gently in his, "Okay, so who's on this list?"

Kevin dimmed the lights on his very excellent new Porsche as he drove up toward Angie's place, parking several houses away from hers. Creeping stealthily from the car, he slunk forward, his head darting cautiously to one side and then another.

Angie opened the door to reveal herself wearing a very sexy and seductive bit of lingerie, music on the stereo almost cartoonishly sexy, but if there was one thing that Kevin could appreciate, it was a sexy cartoon. At the top of the list of his all-time favorite women was Jessica Rabbit. He took in the whole appealing scene with one glance, then distraction set in and he moved toward the window and peered out at the empty driveway beyond. Nope. There was no sign of anything. No assassins, no judges. Kevin thought about the fact that his assailant hadn't actually followed him to this address, so it was unlikely they were out there. Angie's dad on the other hand most certainly was out there, hopefully under the influence of a strong sleeping sedative, but of course Kevin had no way of knowing if that were true.

Angie slithered over to Kevin and from a lovely antique tray offered him the appetizers which she had just made. He took one, popped it into his mouth and ate it absentmindedly, not even remarking on how delicious it was. But so what—she wasn't hosting a garden party.

"I'm so glad you came," said Angie.

"Really? Why?"

Angie looked imploringly at Kevin. "You know why. Because we have something here. Something special. We both know it."

Kevin looked into Angie's eyes then, and saw her sweetness, her vulnerability, her courage in seeking his company despite everything that had occurred recently. She was a lovely girl, seemingly an uncomplicated girl, one to whom he was a desirable commodity, a treasure, unlike the way his wife perceived him. It would be so easy, so pleasant, he thought. Something inside Kevin clicked and he grabbed Angie and began kissing her passionately.

They both sank into the kisses the way a tired, achy person lowers herself into a steaming bubble bath, the scent of pleasure rising all about them, and kisses led to groping and that led to an ensemble stagger toward the bed, where they lay kissing, touching, and beginning to devour each other.

Oh didn't it feel good to be alive, thought Kevin, touching the soft skin of this lovely young girl. Nothing was better than this. This was what made life worthwhile, this sense of newness, of the beginning, the unfolding of the flower. Life was wonderful, and Kevin was alive again. And then a random noise outside distracted him or perhaps for no reason at all, everything went south, well the thing that was supposed to go north did, and beyond that nothing mattered.

And there they sat once again in Angie's bed, covers up to their chins. Kevin pressed his hands to his head for the second time that evening. What had gone wrong? He had a dick that never quit but it had quit. Had he used up all his sex credits? Did he need new batteries? So many bizarre analogies coursed through Kevin's mind as he sat next to a very frustrated young girl. What was he supposed to say? He'd said it before and he said it again.

"Yeah, so if it never happened before, why is it happening with me?" asked Angie. She'd been around and she knew she wasn't supposed to take this personally. This was his issue and it wasn't about her, but it felt personal. She'd been chasing him for so long and now she had him and then what—this. It sucked.

Outside there was the odd sound of dogs barking. Normally the dogs who lived nearby were safely at home, living the respectable lives of pets in this very well-heeled neighborhood. The judge couldn't imagine why it sounded as though his home was being invaded by a choir of canines. He waited, expecting the ruckus to stop, but it only got louder, so he walked to the side of the house from which all the noise was coming, and there outside were several dogs, all of whom scattered when he opened the door and shouted at them, just the sort of reaction he expected from anyone he confronted. He looked down on the ground. What in blazes? There, spread across his entryway was a bunch of half slobbered over lasagna in the very container his daughter had offered him not an hour earlier. He reached down and picked up the container and strode angrily toward her door, pounding loudly on it.

Kevin's eyes opened wide. He glanced at Angie, who still looked irritated. She grabbed a robe as he clutched wildly for his clothes. Where could someone hide in this wide open room? There wasn't enough time to dash toward that bathroom and he couldn't dress rapidly enough, so he wrapped himself in a sheet, and attempted to move around the bed out of sight.

By then Angie had opened the door and was glaring out at her irate father, but for once she met him, cranky glance for cranky glance.

He thrust the half eaten lasagna toward her, saying, "What the hell is the meaning of this?" But before she could even reply, he spotted Kevin and pushed his way into the guesthouse. "You — Julius Caesar — what are you doing here?"

Angie inserted herself between the two men and said defiantly, "He's here to see me. To be with me."

The judge stepped around his daughter a second time and, his eyes flashing, said "I hope it's worth going to jail over. Now get the hell out of here before I have you hauled out of here. You — you — you — doctor of depravity."

Kevin, still wrapped in the sheet, most of his clothes in one hand, but wearing only one shoe and no socks on his feet, saw an opening and dashed through it and out the door without even looking back.

Angie was enraged and for once she would not back down. "You have no right to do this, Daddy, no right."

"The hell I don't. That man belongs in a mental institution."

She stood up taller, her eyes narrowed and boldly she said, "What do you care? It's not like you're interested in any part of my life or me. So what do you care who I fuck?"

Antimangia was visibly taken aback by his daughter's insolence and the sound of that word was like a slap that actually pushed him physically back.

"Yeah, I say fuck. I even do it occasionally," Then under her breath, she mumbled, "Not tonight of course."

The judge looked at her as though she'd suffered some sort of breakdown, then he turned toward the door, but she kept speaking.

Angie walked toward him, her face almost pressed against his as she spat out the words. "Yeah. Get out of here. Go back inside where you belong. I hate you! Hate you! Hate you!"

"My God! That jerk isn't worth all this. Wake up, girl, he's a lunatic."

Angie sneered and seethed. "Oh I hate you all right, and it's not about him. It's about you—you Daddy—you—and all these years of me asking you to look at me, see me, and you waving your hand at me, go away Angie, don't ring the bell Angie, don't walk on the grass Angie. Well, you know what—fuck you."

The judge was stunned and he pressed a hand to his heart, which was beating normally, although it had been wounded deeply.

Angie shouted, "You suck as a dad. You suck!"

The judge shook his head and spoke softly, as if in shock, "I don't know what you're talking about. I'm right here, you're right here. What do you want from me?"

"Nothing, nothing. Go to bed. What's the use. I know you'll never love me. I'm just the fat daughter you'd like to hide in the garage out back."

"Of course I love you. Why would you think I don't love you?"

"Because of the crappy way you treat me — what do you think?"

"Well, my God. I just don't know what to say to that. Don't I have you right here, living right here, where I can see you're safe? Don't I see you every day? Just the other day I was thinking maybe we'd get that dog you said you wanted."

"When I was five? Are you kidding?"

"I could rent this place for a bundle, but do I, of course not. It's so you can be right here."

"Well run an ad, you miserable old fucker. Cause I'm outta here."

Antimangia looked baffled at his daughter. She was hysterical. She needed time to calm down. He'd seen it many times in court. "Get some rest," he said softly, backing out the door, only to have her slam it in his face.

Kevin muttered to himself all the way home. He drove raggedly, a bit unused to the features of the new car, but mostly just distracted by everything. Half thinking, half speaking, he sputtered along, largely unhinged. "It's some sort of devilish retribution. Never thought any harm in doing it. Just a little innocent, okay not so innocent fun, but never hurt anyone. Like a hobby, a casual hobby. My recreation. I deserve it. Now what. I've got a wanker with no wank. A cock with no crow. And what's left for me? Nothing. I'm a eunuch. A life of weighing fat women, nothing more, nothing less. I might as well be dead. I'm already dead below the waist."

Laura heard the car coming when it was still several doors down the block and contemplated putting the chains on the doors, then from the window she saw Kevin emerge from a new car, which irritated her, but then she noticed him all disheveled, wearing one shoe, looking down at his feet, scowling and then tossing the single shoe into the car, all the while clearly frantic and muttering to himself, words she could not hear. This had to be more than the effects of a tryst with Chrissy, so she decided to let him enter the house.

They sat on the stools at the kitchen counter, drinking coffee, although Laura was sure Kevin needed no stimulants this evening, and she listened to the bizarre tale about him being chased all over Sunset Boulevard for days by someone he couldn't identify or catch. Laura considered the most frustrating thing about her marriage the fact that she always knew when Kevin was lying, and she was absolutely certain that tonight he wasn't and so her face softened, the sympathy plainly lit in her eyes. Seeing this look, Kevin put his hand over hers as he continued to speak. At last—someone was listening to him and believing what he'd endured. At last.

Kevin was flooded with love for this woman he'd married so long ago he couldn't even remember why. She was the one person who was always there for him, the one person he could always count on. Why had he been such a fool? "I was dying there, thinking you wouldn't understand, but thank God....Tonight when I couldn't do it, I realized it was time to wake up and come clean. Start over with the one woman I could always trust—with you—here in our beautiful home. Where else would I go, would I belong."

As she began hearing this new line of commentary, Laura's expression started to change, the softness in her eyes faded, she leaned away from him, extricating her hand from under his, but Kevin kept talking, not really observing the nuances of her reactions any longer.

"We're not young any more, not at a place of starting over, no, no way. And so I drove, no raced, over here to you…"

"Tonight when you realized you couldn't do it?" asked Laura. Then with no warning, she slipped down from her stool, gave a mighty shove, and Kevin found himself toppled to the floor, looking up at his enraged wife.

"You know what," she seethed, "I'm angry—furious really, madder than I've ever been. But not at you—I'm pissed at myself."

Hearing this, Kevin jumped up from the floor and took a step toward her, smiling. She said she wasn't mad at him, didn't she?

Laura continued, "For all these years I waited around when I knew there was nothing left. When I knew there was nothing between us, nothing at all. Call a lawyer, Kevin, a good lawyer. And get the hell out of here. Now!"

"Hmm," answered Kevin, "I don't think so."

"I said it's over. Get out."

"Yeah…no. This is my house. You're my wife."

"'Til divorce us do part."

"Not gonna happen."

"Stop it, Kevin. We can have a nice, simple, no contest divorce, or you can go out kicking and screaming and a messy divorce with a witness to your infidelity. The dirty doctor. The press loves that stuff. But will your patients?"

"You wouldn't."

"I might. You don't really know, do you. For all you know, I was the one who got those Honda thugs after you."

Kevin gasped. It couldn't be. "So you admit it!"

"Of course not. But who knows. You know what they say about women scorned. Sometimes we do very rash things."

Kevin looked deep into Laura's eyes. What was there? Was there any information about whether she was lying to him or not? "Stand still, dammit," he said as she turned to dump the coffee from the two mugs into the sink.

"Well, Kevin, as nice as this has been, it's time for you to leave. Get a place. Call a lawyer. I'm sure you'll find a bimbo to screw in roughly twenty minutes. Unless you get mowed down by a Honda. Or maybe they've changed cars too. Maybe they're in a new vehicle and are ready to come at you from any direction. And you won't have a clue until you're rolling down an embankment. Poor, poor Kevin. I just hope that vicious judge doesn't incarcerate you for too long when that happens."

Kevin glowered at Laura. How dare she mess with him like that. Who knew she could be such a scary broad.

It was appalling—and sort of a turn-on. "Okay I'll do you the favor— out of respect for Julie and her security, I'll move into the guesthouse—but only for a while."

"Guesthouse," laughed Laura, "You mean the cabana? You don't remember we remodeled it? There's not even a bed in there."

"There's a bed in the guestroom. And if I had it remodeled, I can have it unmodeled." Kevin marched past his wife and up the stairs and started dismantling the bed in the guestroom and bringing the parts down the stairs while she stood disbelieving, watching him walk up and back.

ELEVEN

When Ben drove up with two other cars tailing him, Angie figured he'd brought some helpers, which made sense, although she was less than thrilled to see that psycho Colette exit a car and race up to Ben for a large and tasteless kiss before they — and Clint, who could lift the world if necessary — entered the guesthouse. It hadn't been difficult to find an apartment and in the last week she'd bought some furniture which had already been delivered. This was really the first time she'd ever set up a home of her own because she'd lived in that guesthouse of her dad's since returning from culinary school. The only things there which she would be moving were clothing, cooking equipment, and books. And the this and that which always must be dealt with during a move.

"Piggylicious!" squealed Colette the moment she saw Angie, grabbing her in an overly long, overly tight hug. "I have a little moving day gift for you." From the depths of her seemingly bottomless tote, Colette dug around and produced a small box wrapped in silver paper, which Angie preferred not to accept but couldn't refuse. It was a small bottle of cologne.

"Orange," said Colette. "I thought it would blend nicely with your natural bacon scent." Angie scowled as Colette continued, "Oh and I brought my tape measure," she said, pulling a tiny dressmaker's reel out of her pocket.

"Oh no, I already have a floor plan, and the furniture is in the apartment, but thanks anyway," said Angie coldly.

"You silly little bacon girl! Does this look like something for a floor plan? It's to measure you—not a wall—for a bridesmaid dress."

Angie looked aghast, and strangely so did Clint, as Ben tried to focus away from the whole scene and on the boxes they'd have to remove.

"I know, I know," said Colette, "If I had my way you'd be maid of honor—always a bridesmaid, never a bride, huh Piggy, but there's my odious cousin Bree—funny you're both named after food..." At that point Ben leaned toward Colette and whispered something in her ear. "Oh my, Ben says I shouldn't call you Piggy, that I'm being rude. Why? Isn't bacon an aphrodisiac? It is to all the men I know."

Then Colette walked even closer and engaged Angie in some sort of intense shoulder lock, her arm wrapped around Angie like a boa constrictor, or at least that's what Angie's expression indicated. "I have the fabric sample right here," and from her tote she extracted some synthetic fabric in a vivid turquoise with bright yellow suns printed on it. "Because you were the light of my sweet Ben's life—'til I came along that is." Colette observed the look of horror on Angie's face, wanted terribly to laugh, but managed to say, "Now I know it's plain, but don't worry, I'm a whiz with a bedazzler."

Angie attempted to toss a desperate glance toward Ben, but he just grabbed a box and headed out to his car. "This place isn't going to empty itself," he said benignly.

"Wait, wait, wait," squealed Colette. "Are you forgetting our rule? Really?"

"Rule?" asked Ben, when he should have been improvising.

"I'm starting to think I should be jealous. You spend ten seconds in the same room with Piggy here and you forget about the magic that is us. What do we never do before we leave a room? We never not kiss. Okay, you've got me all flustered here. Kiss me you fool!"

Ben set the box down, walked toward Colette and reached to peck her cheek but she grabbed him around the neck and kissed him for a very long time.

"If you do that with every box, we'll be moving forever," said Clint seriously.

"Okay," said Colette contritely, "One time special rule. Only for today. Come and go. No kisses." Then she burst into tears while everyone looked on quite stunned. "But it's so tragic, so terribly tragic. What next? We start breaking all our rules at the drop of a hat? What next? Next we'll be sleeping with other people?" She gasped, put a hand over her mouth, and glared at each of the other three in the room. "I never would have believed it of you. Well, Clint, yes I might have suspected you."

"Huh?" said Clint, genuinely baffled.

"Let me be clear right now. There is never going to be any orgies. And my Ben will not be having any free love—not with you missy…" Colette pointed an accusatory finger at Angie and then said "And not with you mister…" and pointed at Clint.

"What?" said Ben and Clint simultaneously with gaping jaws, while Angie just stood and stared at the psycho girl who had somehow entrapped Ben.

"This is a monogamous relationship. We're parents for God's sake. Okay we will be parents. Nobody is cheating, not as cheating or with permission, which be clear on this, there is no permission going around here. Or permissiveness. You get me?"

Ben's eyes lit up with admiration as he looked at Colette. She was kind of a genius. Angie was furious, and that was the whole point. It was working.

When Angie noticed the sparkle in Ben's eyes, she was aghast. It was worse than she'd thought. He really was enamored and the girl was insane. Shouldn't a psychologist be able to recognize that? Was she a patient? Now Angie was really worried.

"We're a little off track here," said Clint good naturedly. "Let's load these boxes, okay?"

In short order they'd finished and Angie looked around. Nothing of hers was left. No more would she be a serf in her dad's world. She was no longer the girl who begged for his attention on a daily basis. She was his ex-daughter. And he could have what he'd always wanted — to be alone and miserable.

They arrived at her new place on Olympic, a nice duplex with two small bedrooms up a winding little staircase in a garden style building. "Nice place," said Ben, "Charming."

Colette strode in and gazed all around then said, "Gee another furnished place huh? Too bad. But you can jazz all this dull stuff up with some paint and fabrics."

"I bought all this furniture," said Angie. "I chose these fabrics."

"Wow how did you and Ben get so close when you're so totally different? This isn't our style at all. Is it Bootylicious Ben?"

Ben glanced behind himself at his nonexistent booty then shrugged. "I think it's very nice," he said.

Colette gasped. "You're choosing her over me? What's going on here? Thursday night—where were you," she asked with venom, pointing at Angie.

"Hey!" said Angie, refusing to take any more, "I grew up with a judge, remember. I don't need you questioning me."

"Aha! So you refuse to answer. I guess we know what's been going on here. It's obvious isn't it? How could you, Ben?"

"Um," said Clint, "What are you talking about?"

"Ben and Angie know what I'm talking about. And so do you. I'm talking about Thursday. Maybe you've heard of it."

"Nothing happened on Thursday," said Ben calmly.

"Sure it didn't. You were just feeding each other bacon. Gnawing each other's spare ribs. Nobody was having raunchy naked pig sex. I just hope you know what you've done and what it's going to take to get me back. Flowers? You're thinking flowers? Well, okay yes I love flowers—you know me very well. But I'm talking way more than flowers. Like blood tests. And you better stay away from that, that, that, bacon bewitcher."

And then Colette turned and stormed out the door.

Ben laughed. "She has lots of personality."

"Yeah—if only she had at least one normal one," said Angie.

"Oh don't worry," said Clint almost seriously, "I've known her for years. She'll get over it."

Bill sat facing Laura at Angie's deli, enjoying their new weekly tradition of meeting there for lunch. He saw the sadness in her eyes despite what she was saying.

"Once I made the decision, it was a relief. I should have done it years ago.... Probably.... You think Julie will handle it okay?"

Bill nodded, "I think so, in time. It's what Candy called the travesty of divorce." He pressed his hand warmly on hers, "I'll be here for both of you."

Laura laughed. "You know you should see him. Every day a delivery comes. A couch, flat screen TV. He put in that outdoor kitchen we always talked about. Giant grill, built in fridge, sink with running water. Julie goes out there every morning and has breakfast with him." Bill was bemused. For a guy who normally was rarely at home, Kevin had hunkered down outside in the cabana. "And you still have a shower out there, right? After the conversion and all?"

Laura nodded. "All the comforts of a first class dorm room. For a third rate idiot.... An idiot who can always crawl back into my heart. Could, I'm changing that to could.... And what about you? Joining the dating game again?"

Bill nodded, "Already started. Candy made a list. Says she can't go to college with me all alone here."

"She's such a trip."

"I think maybe I'm ready now. I was just too desperate to get past the grief, in too much of a hurry. Did you know the kids hated Chrissy?"

"She was just never good enough for you."

"At least she kept me from losing my mind and losing it totally for the kids when I was at my lowest. And now it feels like I'll be okay, funny I guess, but I'm just not as down. I can go on these dates and shrug, say okay we'll see, less urgency."

"Hey that's great."

"Only thing is, it's too easy. I get the sense I could have any one of these women at all, and it's not because of who I am, but what I am."

"Yup, rich doctor, good catch. You could look like a troll, be a troll. No wonder Kevin could screw around so readily."

Bill laughed. "Yeah, he was an innocent bystander in it all."

"Absolutely. Those women were totally at fault. Didn't even unzip his own trousers. He had no choice. Wait—let me wipe away a tear."

"So are you planning to date?"

"Maybe as a way to torture Kevin, like in that movie with the big hut and the little hut. Wow that was an oldie. Match.com? What do you think?"

Bill laughed. "You could date me."

"I think our destiny is to be friends."

Bill hummed, "They're writing songs of love, but not for me...."

Kevin sat on the couch he'd bought for the guesthouse. It wasn't bad, pretty comfortable, and he was fine, but why was he miserable? On the very same Friday, he'd received papers for a dissolution of partnership from Bill and divorce from Laura. From the same attorney, no less. Because he had refused to leave the office, Bill had moved to a new place, taking half the furnishings and equipment and all of the staff, even Caryn, who'd just shrugged when Kevin asked her why she was choosing Bill over him. Without Bill there to generate revenue, Kevin knew the income from the practice would drop severely and the expenses would remain the same. Kevin rebounded quickly and took on a junior associate, which proved to be an excellent idea. This junior doc did more than his share of the work, provided additional billing and received less in compensation. When everything was considered, Kevin knew he would be just fine professionally. He would make a good income, just as he always had. So why was he so miserable? There were several new nurses, all hot, and at least one regularly gave him the eye. He could have her any time he wanted, without Bill there to ruin the fun with his constant disapproval. So why was he so miserable?

There was one and only one thing on Kevin's mind—his wife. He woke in the morning, thinking of Laura. At night before he fell asleep alone in his private little world, it was her face that he saw. He thought about sex and he thought about Laura, but the odd thing was that he thought of them together. When had he last had that sense of yearning for his wife? When had he last felt what could only be described as lust, but no it was more than lust, it was passion, desire, and it wasn't even about the sex. He wanted to go home and Kevin had recognized that Laura was the home he wanted.

It was all so frustrating—he hadn't been like this in years. Every day at lunchtime he called, to say hello to Laura. Sometimes she answered the phone, but rarely did she linger in a conversation. How did it come to be that what formerly was an innocent hobby—chasing after a woman he wanted but wanted only for an hour or two—had devolved into him chasing after his own wife? His life had been upended and it was disorienting and Kevin felt out of sorts on a constant basis. He knew he should have sex—with someone—anyone—just to see if he could do it. His heart filled with terror at the possibility of having that same problem again. At least once a day he thought of taking a drive over to Angie's to see if they could do it at last, but something inside of him said no, and he didn't bother. This was what depression was like. Kevin was depressed, and he knew it.

It was time to face facts—he loved his wife and he wanted her back. Divorce was quick in California—it took only six months. He had to do something now, not linger around wishing things were different. He had to make them different. Kevin knew one thing: he was a charmer, had always been so. There wasn't a woman around who could resist him for long. Hadn't he charmed Laura in the first place, hadn't he stolen her from that guy she was dating after college? And now they were married with a child and a home and on some level she must want to preserve it. He had to step it up, rev up the charm, and make Laura want him again. Surely it wouldn't be that difficult.

Laura was aware of what was on Kevin's mind but she couldn't decide if it was exciting or merely amusing in a kind of pathetic way. When he tapped softly on the kitchen door one night at dinner time, Julie let him in and squealed happily at the heart shaped boxes of chocolates he'd brought for each of them.

"Oh a Valentine!" said Julie.

"The best part is after you eat the chocolate," said Kevin.

"You mean saving the box to put stuff in?" asked Julie, stuffing two pieces into her mouth.

"Dinner is in a few minutes," said Laura, setting her box unopened on the counter. "Only one piece now, Julie."

"I can't just spit it out—that would be rude," said Julie, speaking with her mouth very full of candy.

Kevin laughed. "Nope there's something under the candy."

Julie went scrounging through her box of candy, moving each piece around until she found a little velvet pouch. She quickly popped another piece of candy into her mouth then opened the pouch, which contained a little silver necklace with a tiny heart dangling from it. "Oh wow! Put it on me, put it on me," she said excitedly. After Kevin fastened it around her neck, Julie ran off to look at herself in a mirror.

"Aren't you going to look in yours?" he asked Laura.

"Do you think I'm that easily confused?" Laura replied. She watched as Kevin opened the large candy box and gingerly removed another velvet pouch. From it he spilled into his hand a necklace with a sparkling heart-shaped diamond solitaire. Kevin had very nice hands and very good taste in jewelry.

Laura sighed. "It's beautiful. But I wish you hadn't...."

"I know I've been a jerk and for a long time I haven't acted like much of a husband. I just wanted you to know you're the only woman I've ever given my heart to and you still have it."

Julie ran back in the room before Laura could reply and said, "I'll set a place at the table for Daddy."

"Smells good," said Kevin, looking at Laura.

"Roast beef," said Julie, "Your fave."

Laura sighed again and handed Julie a plate and some silverware.

Kevin thought the dinner had gone pretty well and after Julie had her bath and was tucked into bed, he lingered to talk to his wife. "Thank you for letting me stay," he said rather humbly, "I've missed this so much."

"Julie was happy to have you here," said Laura.

"Only Julie?"

"Go home, Kevin."

"I thought I was."

Laura opened the back door and Kevin morosely walked back to his cabana. It was clear he would have to try harder. Kevin would have to woo his wife, seduce his wife. This was something he could do, something he'd done many times before with many women. It was just harder with a pissed off woman, he knew that, but didn't she have a certain softness in her eyes when she saw the diamond? Kevin thought maybe she did.

Another first date, thought Bill. No wonder everyone hated dating. He didn't actually know if people hated dating but he assumed that must be true. Here he was, in another restaurant, across from another woman, square one. How did people have the time and energy for it? He wondered should he try to become a better sport and consider it more of an adventure. He'd hardly dated at all when he was young, here and there in high school and in his second year of college he'd met JoEllen. Then the dating stopped and real life began. If there were a way now to fast forward past all this crap and resume real life, Bill would be delighted, but hadn't he tried that with Chrissy and look where it had led. At least he'd learned a lesson and had become hyper vigilant. Where before he gravitated toward women who physically reminded him of JoEllen, he was currently so spooked by his year with Chrissy that now he strenuously avoided them.

The current interviewee, as he'd begun calling them, was thus not a pert redhead but a sultry brunette, but perhaps she seemed sultry only because she was so enraged. It started hopefully enough with a mellow exchange about the school soccer program and some laughs about the parent volunteers who'd gone too far overboard about getting high scores and winning the matches.

In the middle of this benign conversation, Erin had looked over Bill's shoulder emitting a staccato gasp, "It's Henry. With a hooker. At this posh restaurant."

Bill discretely turned his head and glanced in the direction Erin indicated but saw only a normal man with one sort of typical Beverly Hills woman, low cut dress, fake boobs, too much jewelry. "I don't think she's a hooker," said Bill.

"Excuse me," said Erin, who rose and marched over to her husband's table and began a conversation that rapidly devolved into a shouting match.

"What are you doing, following me?" shrieked Erin at Henry. "How did you find out where I'd be? Are you hacking my schedule in the computer? Had to hire a hooker to be your beard?"

"Go fuck yourself," said Henry, as people around him looked moderately shocked and extremely annoyed at the shattering of their peaceful dinner hour.

"I'm not a hooker," said the woman, "I'm his attorney."

"Explain the difference," said Erin, staring down the inflated cleavage with a sneer.

"I'm going to have to ask you to leave," said the attorney.

"I'm going to suggest you take makeup lessons at a new clown college," said Erin.

Henry stood and signaled to the waiter to call security.

Bill looked toward the exit of the restaurant with deep yearning. Couldn't he just slip away and pretend he didn't know these people? He needn't pretend—he didn't know them. But then what. He'd surely see Erin at school and leaving her stranded at a restaurant wouldn't be a good idea.

After tossing a glass of wine in her husband's face, Erin returned to the table. Bill could almost see the waves of red, angry light rising from the top of her head as she seethed and spoke of her former husband and the financial tricks he'd been playing on her. This rant went on for quite a while and Bill listened with only half an ear after a short time, although he nodded appropriately. There was no need to ask a question to keep the conversation moving because apparently this woman could continue speaking without stopping for air. Eventually she did stop speaking and just looked at him, clearly waiting for some comment, so he said, "Well love is a battlefield like they say in the song."

"Ah thanks for being so understanding and letting me rant. Say—would you like to come home with me tonight?"

Bill gulped. All he could picture was one of those female insects that during copulation devours the male. "Gosh I can't—kids at home, babysitter, you know. In fact, we'd better get the check."

TWELVE

Butch and Wimp were having a nice lunch at the cute little deli down the street from Zero Tolerance. "Wow," said Butch, "This place is much better than it was the last time we were here."

"Yeah, for sure. I almost didn't want to come here today. So are you ready to hear my news?"

"Ready as rain."

"What? It's not raining." Wimp stood up to look out the window to be sure.

"It's an expression."

"It's right as rain."

"What does that have to do with being ready?"

"So this doctor called in a standing order today — hundred buck bouquet — daily — for his wife — and a two hundred dollar one on Saturday. Sounds like some big time cheating to be atoned for. Wonder how many weeks he'll be good for."

"Well, well aren't you the Mr. Moneybags," said Butch, smiling.

"The business is going very well, but with this windfall, I think it's time."

"For?"

"For me to take you on that trip to India you've always wanted to go on."

Butch sighed with pleasure and reached her hand out to Wimp. "That's fantastic. Look at us. Like an old married couple."

"Yes, we've mellowed. Like those two over there — the perfect couple." Wimp pointed across the deli to Bill and Laura, who were laughing about his recent dates.

"Perfect, exactly," said Butch. "Nobody would hire us to teach him a lesson."

"Nobody hired us to teach anybody a lesson," said Wimp.

"Don't cast aspersions on the mood," said Butch.

At another table Ben sat with Clint, eating panini and jicama slaws. Clint spoke hesitantly, "So how's it going with you and Colette?"

"Oh I just love her," said Ben, smiling. "She's such fun and such a wonderful person."

"Yes, she is," said Clint, "And you love her. Well, I'm happy for you. Sad for me but happy for you."

"Why are you sad?"

"Because oh never mind, just be happy."

"Are we getting confused here?" asked Ben. "Have you forgotten the plan?"

"You mean you and Colette getting married and moving away to have a bunch of babies? No I didn't forget."

Ben laughed. "Wow. I guess we really put that over. It was a ruse, remember, to snap Angie out of her crush on that doctor and realize we're meant for each other."

"But you love Colette now," said Clint.

"You dufus," said Ben. "I do love her, but as a friend. I thought you realized that."

"So I could date her?" asked Clint, visibly cheerier.

"It depends," said Ben. "Is this a one night stand you're looking for like with all the other girls you see or do you care about her and really want to date her?"

"I think I love her," said Clint. "Never felt this way before. Weird. Like being itchy but happy but sad. Well sad cause I thought she was moving away with you. So mainly itchy. Not jock itch or anything."

"I was getting worried there that I'd have to send you to a doctor or something for some industrial strength creams."

"So I can call her?"

Ben laughed and nodded. "Call her. Take her on a nice date."

Angie suddenly appeared at the table. "Who's taking who where?"

"Oh you know Clint," said Ben smoothly, "And it's me taking you, isn't it — still going to the mall aren't we?"

Angie nodded. "Beverly Drive maybe instead of Century City?"

Angie followed Ben to the door, stopping only briefly at Bill and Laura's table. "Everything good?" she asked.

"Fantastic as always," said Bill, smiling.

Angie said, "I'm taking off now but see you next time."

Bill turned to Laura and said, "So do you think I should be keeping some sort of tally or scorecard?"

Laura laughed. "Based on what you're telling me, I'd say scoring is no part of the equation where your dates are concerned."

"I feel so guilty. After every date Candy's there waiting to hear how it went and I have to tell her, sorry little girl, I haven't found you a new mom yet."

"Want me to take her out on a girls' day, with Julie or even just Candy and me? She might like that. Mani-pedi, haircut, stuff like that?"

"That would be wonderful, but sure bring Julie along. No point in her worrying Candy's stealing her mom in the middle of your divorce."

Laura nodded. "Divorce," she said.

"Oh oh," said Bill.

"No, no, not oh oh," said Laura. "Candy and diamonds were bestowed but I still pushed him out the door."

"Sounds like you didn't want to."

"Do you smell that?" asked Laura, "Smoke, coming right in the door. Just a second." Laura dashed out the door only to see a nice looking man standing there reading the riot act to a couple of smokers. He was so strong and confident, so self-assured. Laura couldn't help but admire him.

"This is a restaurant," he said, "People are eating inside. Do you think they want to breathe the disgusting smoke from your cigarettes? Pretty soon Beverly Hills will be a smoke free shopping area just like Santa Monica, at least if I have my way about it. What're you going to do then? Well that's not my problem is it. I can't have you arrested for smoking, but I can for being a public nuisance, so I suggest you put out those cancer sticks and move along. And don't let me see you here again."

The smokers, duly intimidated, put out the cigarettes and hurried away. The judge turned and saw a beautiful woman staring at him and instantly he blushed and said, "Oh please forgive me. I get a little insane about smoking. And this is my daughter's restaurant."

Laura smiled, "Nothing at all to forgive. I came out here to do the same thing. I run an anti-smoking awareness group. Maybe you should volunteer with us."

"I'm Sam," he said, clearly dazzled, and reached out his hand, which Laura took and smiled warmly.

"I'm Laura. Angie's your daughter? She's a lovely girl. And a wonderful caterer."

The judge sighed. "We had a little falling out a couple weeks ago and I've been coming here daily trying to see her and make it up to her, but they keep telling me she's out. I don't think she's ready yet but I really have to apologize."

"She actually did go out—I saw her leave a few minutes ago. But why don't you come in and meet my friend and have a sandwich with us?"

The judge followed Laura inside, and shook hands with Bill as Laura said, "Bill, this is Sam, Angie's dad. He's an anti-smoking crusader too."

Bill laughed. "I guess the world will be tobacco free any day now with both of you joining forces."

"I told Sam to join our group. We need more help, especially with you often too busy to participate."

"I'm a widower with a domineering eight year old who's determined to marry me off to a new mom, and all that dating is a big energy drain but I dare not stop until success is achieved or she'll refuse to attend college."

Sam laughed and looked ruefully up at the ceiling. "I've been in your shoes and wish you lots of luck with that....And what about you," he said, turning to Laura,

"Married, I see." He noticed Laura's wedding ring with what sounded oddly like disappointment.

"Divorcing," said Laura, "Or trying to."

"Her husband has other ideas," said Bill. "Hunkered down in the cabana and wooing her madly. Dated other women all through the marriage but now is wooing only Laura."

"No clue if that's true," Laura said miserably.

"Criminals don't reform that readily," said Sam seriously.

"Oh gosh," said Bill, "I have patients waiting."

"I'm planning to get some take out at the deli counter," said Laura, "So go ahead without me."

Bill reached down to kiss her, shook Sam's hand and raced back to his office.

"Maybe I'm being imprudent and improper," said Sam, "But could I take you to dinner sometime? You did say you filed for divorce, right?"

Laura looked at Sam for a while without speaking. "Okay," she said hesitantly, "Sure. I'd love to have dinner with you. Just don't expect big things."

"You saying yes is already a big thing," said Sam.

It seemed like forever since Angie had some alone time with Ben. Now that he had that odious girlfriend, she was always there, saying or doing something horrendous, thus preventing Angie from telling Ben everything that had happened with Kevin. At last, though, they were alone together, and as they strolled along Beverly Drive, stopping in Crate and Barrel and

Williams-Sonoma, Angie related what had happened as Ben listened hopefully. Then they walked into Pottery Barn toward the back to choose some sheets.

"Yeah," she said, "Old guys are lousy in bed. Who knew?"

Ben smiled encouragingly at her.

"You know," she continued, "I realized it wasn't just an older man thing. It was the thrill of being found out—like you know—those people who have sex in public. Can you believe that?"

Ben pondered only for a moment what she'd just said then answered, "You'd have thought after what happened with your law professor, enough would've been enough."

Angie laughed. "I haven't thought of him in ages." Her mind wandered back in time to when she was pre-law in college and had a massive crush on darling Professor Wanamaker, who was over fifty at least, a tiny little firecracker of a guy, although as she looked back now, he seemed more nebbishy than dynamic. It was so strange how people looked different in recollection than they had during the actual moment.

She was extremely overweight in those days and leaned over him as he pointed to a passage in a thick law book. As soon as he felt her breast graze his forearm, he snapped around, stood, and pressed against Angie, bending her back against the desk. How funny to remember him and how small he was. Angie felt like a giant next to him, both in height and girth—how unpleasant that was. But then he was kissing her and sliding his hand up her skirt, well trying to because it was way too tight and provided much resistance. As his hand struggled north, Angie moaned.

Yanking and tugging at her too-tight clothing, the professor valiantly kissed her neck, throat, and breast, battling all the while with the determined skirt and mumbling his far from aphrodisiacal version of thinking about baseball to prevent an early finish, "Corpus Juris Secundum...the right to a speedy and public trial, being twenty-one years of age, and citizens of the United States, or in any way abridged, except for participation in rebellion, or other crime...."

Unaware that the door was opening, the professor kept kissing, tugging, and mumbling until a cough came from the doorway, causing him to snap to attention and back off from Angie. It was the dean, who sternly said, "Professor!"

It had a very unhappy ending. Angie recalled loading her car with suitcases and boxes and driving away, college in the background, as a small group of students angrily marched in front of the dean's office, holding signs demanding that the dean reinstate Professor Wanamaker.

Angie sighed. "Yeah, maybe, but do you really think I belonged in pre-law?"

She reached for a packet of nice sheets and wanted to feel the fabric, but Ben pulled her behind a display, took a deep breath and kissed her deeply. Angie was stunned but kissed him back. Emboldened, Ben held her even more tightly and kissed her with increasing fervor. Then he reached down and began unbuttoning her blouse.

Angie leapt back from Ben and looked at him, shocked, "Someone could see!"

"I thought that was what you wanted," said Ben.

"Wait a second," said Angie, pausing to think. "No, no, it's not."

"It's me," said Ben, by now quite miserable. "Or I should say it's never been me, never will be me. You just don't want me."

"No, it's not about you."

"Obviously."

"Wait….I get it! It was them getting caught. I wanted them to get punished. These older guys—older guys like my…."

"Father!" said Ben.

Suddenly Angie turned to look at Ben, and this time she actually saw him. Her eyes opened wide, and she pulled him to her, wrapped her arms around his neck and kissed him. And she kissed him. And kissed him. She stopped only for a moment to ask, "What about Colette?"

"Don't worry about her. Let's go to your place and I'll tell you all about it. After," said Ben.

"After," said Angie, sighing sweetly.

– THIRTEEN –

The judge had decided that he would just go over to Angie's new apartment instead of barging into her deli every single day. At least she'd have to come home at some point and finally they would talk. He'd just sit there at her door for as long as necessary. He thought about bringing her flowers but he knew such a cheesy gesture wouldn't mean that much. And it wasn't as though he could bake her a cake. All he had to offer her was words, and he knew they were long overdue.

Inside the apartment, Angie lay snuggled in bed next to Ben, deep in a sweet afterglow. For the first time in her entire life she felt safe and truly happy. And how she'd laughed when he told her about Colette's scheme to snap her out of her trance. "I guess we'll have to double date," laughed Angie, "Maybe at a barbecue place. At least now I don't have to shop for a deodorant that masks the smell of bacon."

Ben laughed. "I'd love you even if you smelled like pig feet."

"Pigs' feet are a delicacy."

Ben grimaced and said, "Good to know."

When the bell rang, Angie and Ben said simultaneously, "Pizza!" She grabbed a robe and headed toward the stairs as he scrambled for his clothes. "You can stay in bed," she said adorably.

"I can undress again. No point in dripping pizza on your new sheets."

"Romantic," said Angie, laughing as she dashed down the stairs and opened the door, still chuckling. It wasn't pizza though, it was her dad.

"Please let me talk to you," he said sincerely.

"This isn't a good time," said Angie, her voice cold. "I'm not alone."

The judge pushed his way in the door. "That maniac isn't here, is he?" But it was Ben who came down the stairs in just trousers, no shirt, no shoes, no socks.

Angie looked nervously at her father. Would he now go all berserk on Ben?

Instead Sam's face lit up, and he strode smiling toward Ben, and reached out for what Ben assumed to be a handshake but instead the judge crushed him in a massive hug. "Thank God," he said, "Thank God. I've hoped you two would get together for years."

"Since when have you hoped anything about me other than that I'd go away," said Angie frostily.

Sam reached out and took his daughter by the hand and said, "Please sit and listen to me."

"I'll give you some time alone," said Ben, rushing up the stairs before Angie could say anything.

"I wish I had a good explanation or something cathartic to say," said Sam, "But what excuse do I really have? When your mother left, I allowed myself to put a wall around my heart and was too lazy to knock it down. Pathetic, I know. You're my daughter and I love you so much, but for years I've tried to avoid feeling anything and it just got easier to be an old crank instead of a nice person. But it wasn't about you at all."

"Nothing has ever been about me," said Angie. "Wolves do a better job raising humans than you did."

"Yes. I'm so sorry. I wish I hadn't hurt you. I wish…. But look at how fantastic you turned out. You're this sweet, loving, kind, generous girl, a big success, and everyone loves you. If only I could take credit, say I must have done something right, but maybe this is just you being you. And I'm proud of you, really so proud of how you turned out and all you've accomplished."

Angie started to cry. "But why didn't you ever say so? It would have meant so much to me."

"I was an asshole. But I'm saying so now, if that means anything at all."

Angie sobbed and said nothing.

"When you said those things to me it was like a shock to my heart and maybe it knocked that wall down, I don't know. I had no idea you felt that way, Angie, really. And that's my fault too. I should have been looking and listening, not figuring if you were right outside the door and physically safe, everything was all right, you were all right. What a jerk, huh. I can take care of plants but not the person I love best in the world. I just hope you'll give me another chance. See me now and then. I know I don't deserve it. I'm a terrible person. But I want to be a better person. And a better dad. And I never wanted you to be hurt. And that will stay with me for the rest of my life."

"Yeah," she laughed, "Shovel on the guilt."

"Finally—Catholic school comes in handy."

The bell rang again and Angie rose. "Pizza," she said.

"Well I'll go and let you kids eat. Maybe think about what I said? Maybe have dinner with me some time."

"Ack," she said, "Sit. Eat some pizza. That's what families do."

"But it's a nice day, a lovely day, so just think of it as we're going out for a drive on the way to the movies," said Wimp to Butch. "It's just around the corner here."

"We had a healthy, happy, perfectly defined relationship for years, then suddenly you decide to break with tradition and now you're telling me what to think and where to turn? Suddenly I'm your driver?"

"You're driving me crazy, I can tell you that."

Butch gasped. "Tomorrow, mister. Getting a new crop. Things have gone too far."

"You've gone too far."

Butch gasped once again. "You've crossed the line this time and strangulated my patience with it."

"No, I mean you passed the house. It's the one back there with all the gardening going on."

Kevin was outside in his front yard, overseeing a small battalion of gardeners who were planting rows of rose bushes according to his design. The flowers had been well-received but Laura still had not relented. In fact, she had gone out several times in the last few evenings, leaving him alone with Julie. At least once again he'd had the pleasure of sitting in his den, watching his own television, and being at home with his child. The question was, where had Laura been going? It seemed too unlikely to assume she'd been dating, and besides she was always home before ten at night. But what if she were dating? What if she'd found someone else? Day by day Kevin grew more desperate. He had to know Laura would take him back so that his life could resume. He wanted to live in his own home with his family.

Today while she was dropping Julie off on a sleepover, he was out in the yard conveying his design scheme to gardeners who couldn't seem to follow what he wanted. "Look, he said for the fifth time, "Dark pink, pale pink, white. Then pale pink, dark pink, pale pink, white. See?" The gardeners nodded and then proceeded to set the plants down in random order. Kevin repeated the simple phrase in Spanish and they nodded and did the same thing. Finally he held up an exasperated hand and indicated he would lay them out. In short order he had placed the several dozen rose bushes along the picket fence that bordered his front yard. Satisfied with what he had created, he nodded toward the gardeners and indicated they could now plant everything.

Butch had made the obligatory U-turn and pulled up to the curb as Wimp exited the car carrying the Saturday bouquet for the doctor's wife. Wimp hoped she never took the fool back because his income had increased so much as a result of this doctor's floral peacemaking efforts.

Butch remained in the Honda, rapping her fingers on the steering wheel and thinking about different types of handcuffs, when she noticed Kevin walking toward one of the gardeners to discuss what was being planted. Didn't he look familiar? Didn't she know him? All of a sudden, her hand rose and clapped against her mouth. Bill! That was Bill! Urgently Butch honked the horn and gestured for Wimp to come immediately.

Kevin watched with some satisfaction as yet another bouquet was set at the front door. He started to walk toward the delivery guy to tip him when a horn blasted several times so he turned toward the curb and spotted the vehicle parked there. Honda CR-V. It was the Honda! Kevin was certain of it. He strode purposely toward the car but somehow the delivery guy had leapt into the front seat and the car had sped away.

Kevin raced to the garage, jumped into his Porsche and blasted down the street after the Honda. He was sure he could catch them, assuming they hadn't turned.

Butch was determined to practice evasive maneuvers and she had indeed turned, several times and had doubled back and turned again.

Wimp was too distraught even to express fright at the way Butch was driving, for there was a more compelling source of terror at the forefront of his mind. "He knows who we are! He saw me dropping off the flowers. He can come into the shop! With les gendarmes!"

"What arms? You think he has guns?"

"Police, the police. Oh my God." Wimp pictured himself locked away, in chains and not the good kind. Not the consenting adults kind. The only one adult is consenting and the other adult is somebody's bitch kind. He started moaning softly and raising his hands to his head.

Butch's voice grew eerie, "I looked right into his eyes for a moment—pure evil. I bet he's one of those plural marriage guys—house with a wife on every corner—what are they called—Amish. They get married to so many women because they're not allowed to watch TV."

"You don't think it's credit card fraud, do you? I'd have to refund the money—and I already spent so much of it on the tickets. But no—we'll go—they'll never catch us. We'll seek asylum in India."

"I'll be dammed if anyone is committing me. Electro shock therapy? No thank you very much." Butch sped up and quickly turned onto and then off Sunset, looking to each side, and in her rearview mirror, but there was no sign of the Porsche.

Kevin's rage escalated. How had they escaped? How had they been fast enough in that damn Honda to evade his chase? Was it a magic Honda with some sort of cloak of invisibility? Were they freaking Batman? He'd lost yet another chance to apprehend them. Oh he'd been so close to catching them and imagine the fallout if he could have done that and had called the police and finally got his justice—that moron cop and moldy judge would finally get their comeuppance. What utter frustration. Why had his life gone to shit? Day by day he struggled with all these problems, and so far no reward. No wonder he didn't believe in God.

Kevin drove back home resignedly to tell Laura about what had happened, and yes there was her car, parked in the driveway and alongside it—the Honda CR-V. Kevin's eyes bulged and his nose flared. Had Laura in fact been the one to sic these maniacs on him? Were they now blackmailing her? Or were they all conspiring further? After all he'd done for her, too. She was shameless. No, that was too crazy to believe.

Kevin parked behind Laura and barreled into the house ready to confront the car's owner only to find her talking and laughing with that rabid judge. "My God!"

shouted Kevin, "This is unbelievable. What are you doing here in my house?" He strode menacingly up to the judge and stood nearly nose to nose. "You have no jurisdiction here."

Sam turned to Laura and said, "This clown is your ex-husband?"

"Kevin," said Laura, "This is my friend, Sam."

"You're in my house, asshole, and this is my wife. Get out of here or I'll be the one calling the cops."

"Stop it, Kevin. Stop it immediately. I'm sorry, Sam, really. What's the matter with you?"

"Just because she threw me out and filed for divorce doesn't mean this isn't my house and she isn't my wife," asserted Kevin.

Sam displayed his most judicial countenance and said, "That's exactly what it means. Laura, I can get you a restraining order today if you like."

"Restrain this," said Kevin, socking the judge on the jaw. "You catch me with your daughter and so you come here trying to snake away my wife? She's my wife, pal. I'm keeping her."

Laura pushed her way between Kevin and Sam and turned to her husband with rage and said "Angie....That sweet young girl? A patient. And basically a kid. No wonder she switched to Bill."

"Don't be so smug," Kevin said, "She was coming onto me for months. I asked Bill to take her case. And nothing happened with her. I was being run off the road, remember. And you hung up on me so she gave me a ride."

"Kevin, I told you this weeks ago but I was never genuinely sure until this moment. It's over. You need to get your stuff and move out of the cabana. Get a place of your own. Build a new life of your own. I'm never taking you back."

"You heard the lady," said Sam. "I'm not leaving until I see you drive away from here. I'll file that restraining order and post a policeman if necessary. You can't be a sleaze ball and keep a fantastic woman like this."

"This isn't over," said Kevin to Laura, and then more softly, "I'll never give up on you—I finally know what you mean to me. I want to make it up to you for the rest of my life."

"Make it up to someone else," said Laura. And pointing toward the door, "Go. If you don't go, I will get that restraining order. Today. Immediately. Enough of these games." She watched as Kevin padded out the door, his head down and shoulders slumped.

When the door was closed, Laura turned toward Sam, "Oh God, look at your face. Wait, let me get you some ice."

"No," said Sam, "You wait. I was holding off on doing this until you were sure about your marriage. You seem pretty sure today." As if in slow motion, he reached toward her, enveloped her in his arms, and gently reached down and kissed her for a very long time.

Butch and Wimp sat in the international terminal at LAX airport. He clutched her hand tightly. "I was one payment away from owning that car," Butch said morosely. "It would have lasted fifteen more years, maybe twenty."

"Prison isn't like college," said Wimp sagely, "They don't let you bring your car. Destroying the plates and abandoning it was the only choice we had. The insurance will pay off and you'll get a new one. And you won't be in jail."

"You don't know Bill would come into the shop. He didn't come in to place the order. Maybe a secretary did it."

"And what, she got amnesia over night?" Wimp scowled at Butch.

"Maybe a vicious sister wife did it and she won't tell."

"The car is gone. Make peace with it. We're going on vacation. Let's just try to get our sanity back and when we come home this will all be a distant memory. And you'll get a new car. Maybe a nice Toyota," said Wimp comfortingly.

"Now you're just trying to depress me. Oh look, isn't that Guru Magic — that Indian Guru — very famous."

Wimp turned to look at a group of Indian women, all in brightly colored saris, following behind a woman who did have a certain spiritual countenance. "Oh my God," he said, "Never mind the guru — look at the girl in pink. The pale pink."

"So? I really don't think she's the kind to recruit for any threesomes."

"Chrissy!" he whispered.

"Oh my God, it is her. Wow she got fat. How many pounds do you think?"

Wimp shrugged. "Gotta be twenty or thirty. Woah how could she gain so much so fast?"

"Curry?"

"She's seeking asylum in India too. How about that. Do you think she'll be on our tour? That could be awkward." Wimp mulled this over. At least there was no sign of Bill. "Oh my God, do you think Bill is here?" Wimp held his hands over his face and rose, peering in every direction, then grimaced at Butch and sat back down. "No sign of him."

"Maybe they're not gurus but all Bill's wives, a coven or something. A whole herd of wives, running away," said Butch. "It's about time someone taught him a lesson. Who's gonna do his laundry now?"

Candy pulled Bill aside and said seriously, "You really have to talk to Will. He can't use his manners tonight."

Bill laughed and asked, "What's wrong with him using manners?"

"He only has bad ones," said Candy. "And our cousins will be here."

"What?" said Bill. "Aunt Ruth didn't tell me she was coming for a visit."

"Not those cousins." Candy gestured toward next door, saying "The cousins we've never met. They're coming to the party."

"I know how much you love Mrs. G," said Bill, "But you do know we're not actually related to her, right? And her grandkids aren't your cousins."

"Please!" said Candy with visible exasperation. "Is this really the time for that kind of talk?"

Bill laughed.

"Now's the time to focus. I need you to take my pictures with your cell phone and put them on the computer."

"Pictures?" asked Bill.

"I have to try on some outfits and need to know which looks best. So that way I can look at all the pictures and decide."

"Where'd you get a crazy idea like that?"

"Duh!" said Candy, "*Clueless* of course."

"Don't you have a new dress just for the party? Didn't Aunt Laura take you shopping and get you a bunch of stuff?"

"Daddy! You're lollygagging around, not even dressed, Will for all we know is up to his ears in slime, and I'm the only one paying attention and now you want to discuss shopping? Focus, Daddy, focus!"

Bill shrugged, "Okay, go put on the outfits. Camera right here."

While Candy was dressing, Will appeared, saying, "What?"

"What what?" asked Bill.

"Candy said you wanted me."

"That kid will end up president one day," muttered Bill. "You ready for the Gold's anniversary party? Better get dressed."

"It's an outside party. I am dressed."

"It's a garden party, yes, but not a jeans party. Go put on nice slacks and a clean shirt."

"Oh, crap," said Will.

After the normal amount of nagging on Candy's part, grousing on Will's part, and some relief on Bill's that he could once again fit perfectly into his clothes, they walked together across the lawn to the Gold's back yard, Bill carrying a large box containing a nice present onto which Candy had taped a card she'd drawn herself.

"Remember Will, try not to make anyone hate you right away," admonished Candy.

"Nobody hates me but you," Will answered.

"I'm the only one who really knows you," said Candy.

"Stop it," said Bill sternly. "Nobody hates anybody."

"Gramma!" shrieked Candy as Sophie walked over to greet them. "Happy Anniversary!"

"Thank you! You put in your time and you get the good stuff," said Mrs. G, holding out her arm to show off a new diamond tennis bracelet.

"Bling!" said Candy. "So, where are these cousins?"

Sophie laughed and said to Bill, "Could you put that inside? There's a table near the kitchen. Never expected so much loot."

Bill laughed and nodded as the kids followed behind Mrs. G toward a group of youngsters playing at the back of the yard.

The house was quiet and seemed to be empty, but as Bill went to set his gift upon a table that was about to overflow, he heard someone enter, but didn't look up. "This could be the straw that breaks this table," he joked.

"Maybe we'd better designate this coffee table for the overflow," a woman's voice said, and as Bill looked up to see who she was, she lifted a large bowl from the table and turned with it and walked out of the room.

Bill felt something inside him flutter, a feeling he hadn't felt in a very long time. He walked toward the door where she'd gone and followed her down a hallway to the living room. He watched her set the bowl down on a table in there and then she turned and faced him. She was not that tall but reasonably slender, her hair dark and shining, with the perfect amount of freckles spattered across her nose.

The flutter. Again. Remembering that feeling, without hesitation he walked toward her. As he moved forward, Bill felt something inside his heart change, as though a cog that once had slipped, just now dropped back into place. Inside him all was humming. With each of the few steps that separated them, he could feel himself walking into a future that would last forever, that he had finished the past, had left the present, and now was moving into what would become his ever after.

Her eyes flashed and sparkled and she said, "Oh, you're Bill. Mom said I'd meet you. I'm Gigi."

"Of course," he said, "Gigi." He smiled and opened his arms, and without hesitation, she walked right into them. "How about that," he murmured, "Twice in a lifetime."

ABOUT THE AUTHOR

Nancy Frederick was born in Brooklyn, New York, raised in New Jersey and Florida and has been an uneasy California transplant for the last couple of decades. She's an internationally acclaimed astrologer who is the author of thousands of articles and six New Age books. When she's not doing readings for clients across the globe, she's writing novels, of which this is her most recent. She enjoys strolling outside in the beautiful California sunshine, going to movies, and cooking. She's @NancySussan on Twitter.